"If we don't comply with the condition he set down, we'll be giving certain members the opportunity to acquire enough stock to take over control of the company. I've no intention of allowing that to happen either."

The pause was brief. "Which reduces the options to just the one."

Ross studied her for a lengthy moment or two, still giving little away. When he spoke again it was with a certain calculation.

"It won't be a long-term marriage. There's nothing to stop us divorcing after everything is settled. In the meantime, we both live our own lives. I'd continue to run the company, of course. You needn't be involved. All I'd ask is that you sell me enough shares to make up the fifty-one per cent for overall control."

*Legally wed,
But he's never said…
"I love you."*

*They're…*

The series where marriages are
made in haste…and love comes later….

Look out for more WEDLOCKED! wedding
stories available only from Harlequin Presents®:

*The Disobedient Bride*
by Helen Bianchin
May #2463

*The Moretti Marriage*
by Catherine Spencer
June #2474

# Kay Thorpe
# THE BILLION-DOLLAR BRIDE

Wedlocked!

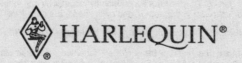

# HARLEQUIN®

TORONTO • NEW YORK • LONDON
AMSTERDAM • PARIS • SYDNEY • HAMBURG
STOCKHOLM • ATHENS • TOKYO • MILAN • MADRID
PRAGUE • WARSAW • BUDAPEST • AUCKLAND

ISBN 0-373-12462-7

THE BILLION-DOLLAR BRIDE

First North American Publication 2005.

www.eHarlequin.com

**Printed in U.S.A.**

# CHAPTER ONE

SHE had imagined someone older. Ross Harlow was almost certainly no more than the mid-thirties. The bronzed, hard-boned features were surmounted by thick dark hair crisply styled. Six feet two, she calculated, and well-honed beneath the superbly cut suit.

Grey eyes swept her from head to toe and back again, revealing little in the process. Gina pulled herself together to extend a hand in formal greeting—aware of a warm trickle down her back as long lean fingers closed briefly about hers.

'How is…my grandfather?' she asked.

A muscle contracted along the firm jawline. 'As well as can be expected, I guess.' His glance took in the single leather suitcase on the trolley. 'Is this everything?'

'I wasn't planning on staying long,' she said. 'I might not be here at all if my parents hadn't urged me to come.'

'Good of them.'

Green eyes acquired a spark. 'They're good people.'

His shrug was dismissive. 'I'm sure. I've a car waiting.'

He took the suitcase from the trolley, leaving the latter where it stood in the middle of the arrivals hall as he headed for the exits. Gina had to run to keep up with his lengthy stride. His attitude left a lot to be desired, though she could to a certain extent understand his feelings. She was more of a Harlow than he could ever be.

The limousine parked in the 'no waiting' zone was long and black. A uniformed chauffeur got from the driving seat on their approach, and opened the rear door for her.

Feeling distinctly queen-like, Gina slid onto soft cream leather, feet sinking into the thick carpeting. Not the type of transport she would have imagined a man as essentially masculine as Ross Harlow might favour, but then who was she to judge? This was a different world. A world way outside her experience.

The chauffeur took her suitcase from Ross to put it in the boot, leaving him to slide into the rear seat beside her. He pressed some hidden switch, bringing a glass panel sliding smoothly up from between front and rear seats to cut them off from the driver.

'I gather you're adopted yourself,' Gina said with some deliberation as they pulled out.

The dark head inclined. 'I was fourteen when my mother married Oliver, my sister nine. He gave us both his name.'

'Your natural father didn't object?'

'My mother was widowed.'

'I'm sorry.'

'You don't need to be. Oliver's been a very good husband to her, and an excellent father to Roxanne and me.'

'Better than to his own daughter,' Gina felt moved to state. She shook her head as he made to speak. 'I know she's no longer alive. The letter he sent explained everything. It was his insistence that she gave me up at birth. His wife at the time—my grandmother—died the year after Jenny was killed on the road. He married your mother two years later.'

Ross regarded her for a moment in silence, his expression curious. 'You seem remarkably cool about it all.'

'I don't see any point in crying over something twenty-five years in the past,' she returned. 'My parents are wonderful people. I've had a very good life with them.'

'Assuming you knew you were adopted before receiving

Oliver's letter, you must have wondered about your real parents.'

'Occasionally,' she admitted. 'But never with any intention of looking them up. We moved to England when I was just a few months old, so I'd no memories to disturb me.' She paused, collecting her thoughts. 'The letter said nothing about the man who fathered me.'

Ross lifted his shoulders. 'It seems Jenny would never say who he was.' His regard centred on her face beneath its crown of honey-blonde hair, appraising the deep green eyes, small straight nose and soft full mouth. 'I saw a photograph once. You look very much like her.'

There was no denying the pang that statement elicited. Gina shook off the momentary heartache. It was too late to go down that road. What was done was done. What she had to deal with was the present.

'Did you know she'd once had a child?' she asked.

He shook his head. 'The first I knew was when Oliver told me he'd contacted you.'

'It must have been a real shock.'

'It was all of that,' he agreed drily.

'I'm not here to make any claims, if that's your concern,' she said. 'I'm more than satisfied with what I already have.'

'I understand you own a boutique.'

She turned a deaf ear to suspected disparagement. 'Part own. Hardly on a par with the Harlow empire, but enough to keep me both occupied and solvent. I stayed in one of your hotels once,' she added blandly. 'Very nice.'

Ross's lips twitched. 'We do our best. You'll be staying at the house, of course.'

'Your mother has no objection to that?'

'None that I'm aware of.'

'Do you live there too?' she asked after a moment, and saw the faint smile come and go again.

'I have the penthouse suite in our Beverly Hills concession.'

'Some bachelor pad!'

He gave her a quizzical glance. 'What makes you think I'm unmarried?'

'We spinsters have a sixth sense about such things.'

This time the smile held a genuine if fleeting humour. 'Never met anyone *you* fancied marrying?'

'I prefer independence too,' she returned. 'For now, at any rate.'

They had left the airport environs and were travelling along a multi-lane freeway, with the city spread out in all directions. Los Angeles. Her birthplace. Gina still found it hard to take in.

'Where are we heading for?' she asked.

'Mullholland.' Ross indicated the line of hills ahead. 'Oliver prefers to live above the smog-line.'

'You always call him by his name?'

'It's the way he wanted it. From me, at any rate. Roxanne calls him Dad.'

'How did your sister take the news?'

'Badly,' he said. 'She's accustomed to being the baby of the family.'

Gina did a swift calculation using the figures she'd been given a few minutes ago. Ross had to be thirty-four now, his sister twenty-nine. Some baby!

'Married?' she hazarded.

'Divorced. A hazard in these parts.'

'The reason you haven't tried it yourself yet?'

'Maybe a part of it.' He studied her a moment, an unreadable expression in his eyes. 'You're not what I expected.'

'Is that good news,' she asked, 'or bad?'

His grin was unexpected. 'I'll take a raincheck.'

Gina relaxed a little, glad to have the atmosphere lightened. Meeting her grandfather for the first time, knowing he was dying, wasn't going to be easy, but she'd get through it. All he wanted, he'd said, was to see her before he died—to hear from her own lips that he was forgiven for what he'd done. She could give him that in the circumstances, even if it wasn't entirely true.

The Harlow residence was reached via a winding canyon road affording panoramic views at every bend. Double iron gates, electrically controlled, gave access to a drive and forecourt backed by a house big enough to house a dozen families. White stone walls glowed in the late-afternoon sunlight, outlined against a sky already deepening in hue. A riot of colour met the eyes in every direction.

The chauffeur drove through an archway to bring the car to a stop before a bank of garages built into the hillside. A further archway revealed a wide, bow-fronted terrace affording another superb view over the city, marred only by the smog-line smudging the horizon.

They entered the house via impressive double doors into a vast circular hall floored in marble. A beautifully wrought-iron staircase curved up one wall to an open gallery. The crystal chandelier dropping from a central support high up in the glass-roofed atrium was breathtaking in its size and beauty, the light from above sparking myriad colours.

If the woman who appeared from one of the rooms leading off the hall was Elinor Harlow, she had to be in her mid-fifties at least, Gina reckoned, but it was a very well-preserved mid-fifties. Her dark hair was immaculate, her face beautifully made-up, her figure hourglass in an off-white gown that shouted designer wear.

'It's easy to see you're Jenny's daughter!' she exclaimed. She came forward swiftly to take Gina's hand in hers, her smile warm. 'This means so much to my husband! He bitterly regrets the way he acted all those years ago. If you can find it in your heart to forgive him…'

'I do,' Gina assured her. 'That's why I'm here.'

'Where is he?' Ross asked.

'Asleep at the moment.' A cloud passed across her face. 'He hasn't been too good at all today.'

'He'll rally.' Ross sounded confident about it. 'He always does. In the meantime, Gina might like to freshen up.'

'I'll show you your room,' Elinor offered. 'Michael will bring your bags up.'

'One bag,' Ross put in. 'Unlike some I could mention, this lady travels light.'

His mother pulled a face at him. 'I believe in covering all eventualities, darling. Who can ever tell what might be needed?'

Gina followed her up the curving staircase, conscious of the grey eyes watching her climb. She was relieved to reach the gallery.

'It's a beautiful house,' she commented. 'And so huge!'

Elinor laughed. 'It's considered on the smaller side by Mullholland standards. You should see the Gregory place further along the road. Now. *that* is really some size! It's said Valentino once owned it.' She opened a door. 'Here you are. I hope you'll be comfortable.'

The bedroom was as large as Gina's whole flat back home, the bed raised on a carpeted platform in the centre and draped in cream silk to match the window dressings, the furnishings exquisite.

'I'm sure I shall,' she said, controlling the urge to express further admiration. This was the way these people lived. Nothing unusual to them.

'Dinner isn't until eight,' Elinor added, 'but I can have something brought up to you if you're hungry.'

'I'm fine,' Gina assured her. 'I ate on the plane. The first time I've travelled first class. I'm not sure I'll ever be able to settle for economy again!' she added jokingly.

'I doubt if you'll ever have to,' the older woman said easily. 'Come on down when you're ready. You'll find us on the top terrace.'

Gina bit her lip, suspecting that the remark might have been misconstrued. She wanted no financial reward for making this trip. She was here to offer some comfort to a dying man, nothing else.

The *en suite* bathroom was a symphony in black and cream, the bath sunken and complete with jacuzzi, the walk-in shower cabinet walled with jets in addition to a vast overhead spray. She came back to the bedroom to find her suitcase laid ready on the stand at the foot of the bed, although she hadn't heard anyone enter the room.

The simple black dress she extracted to hang out was adaptable to any of the eventualities Elinor had mentioned. Not designer wear exactly, but capable of holding its own. Not that she had any desire to compete. She wanted no part of this world of theirs. In fact, the sooner she got back to her own world the better.

Dropped on her right out of the blue, the letter from her grandfather had caused upheaval for both her and her parents. He'd had her traced, he'd said, because he couldn't bear to go to his grave without making some attempt to right the wrong he had done her. She hadn't wanted to come, but the nature of the plea had made it impossible to refuse outright.

It was still only a little gone seven when she made her way downstairs again. With no sign of anyone to ask directions of, she chose one of the doors leading off from the hall, to find herself in what was obviously a formal dining room. The gleaming mahogany table was unset, the heavy silver candlesticks devoid of candles, the whole ambience one of occasional rather than general use.

'Can I help you, ma'am?' asked a voice at her back, and she turned to see a middle-aged man dressed in a conservative grey suit.

'I'm looking for a way out to the upper terrace,' she said. 'I'm...'

'I know who you are, ma'am.' The tone was courteous, his expression neither friendly nor unfriendly. 'If you'll come this way.'

Gina followed him a little uncertainly. The term of address he had used suggested a member of staff rather than family.

'You are?' she asked.

'Alex, ma'am,' he said without turning his head. 'Mr Harlow senior's personal aide.'

He proffered no further information, and she was loath to ask him how her grandfather was. She had the impression that the man no more approved of her presence here than Ross Harlow himself. At least Elinor had extended a welcome.

The house had been deliciously cool. Stepping out onto the wide span of the terrace was like stepping into a furnace, even this early in the year. She was thankful to see the umbrellas shading the tables and loungers set about the paved surface.

Ross Harlow was seated alone at one of the former. He was minus his suit jacket, the sleeves of his cream shirt rolled to reveal tanned forearms. His feet were lifted to rest comfortably against a lower rail of one of the other chairs, one hand about to raise a glass to his lips.

He got up when he saw her, surveying her appearance without comment. 'How's the jet lag?'

'So far, not bad,' Gina acknowledged. 'Surprising, considering it must be close on three in the morning back home.'

'It's always best to try adjusting right away to the time,' he said. 'What would you like to drink?'

'I'll have a Kir, please.'

Ross passed on the request to the man waiting by the wide glass doors through which they'd emerged. Staff demarcation lines didn't appear to be strictly observed, Gina reflected. She took the seat Ross drew out for her, watching him from beneath her lashes as he regained his own seat. Seen in profile, his jawline was firm, a hint of implacability in its set.

'Are you staying for dinner?' she asked.

'I am,' he returned. 'Mother should have told you we only bother dressing for formal occasions. Not that you don't look delightful.'

'Thanks,' she said, refusing to be embarrassed about it. 'As *my* mother would say, when in doubt opt for a compromise. I refrained from putting my hair up.'

Humour briefly lit the grey eyes again. 'You certainly inherited the Harlow quickness of tongue. I've never known Oliver stuck for an answer either.'

'When do I get to see him?' she asked.

'In the morning. He doesn't feel up to it tonight.'

Brows drawn, it was a moment before she could put the question. 'How long does he have?'

The shrug was brief, eyes veiled. 'A few weeks. Maybe more, maybe less. He's a resilient character.' His tone altered a fraction. 'I hope you're not planning on hauling him over the coals when you do see him.'

'Of course not.' She controlled the urge to snap with an

effort. 'I told you before, it's in the past. I'll be on a flight home in a couple of days.'

Ross studied her for a moment or two. 'A hell of a way to come for a couple of days,' he remarked at length.

'I don't see any point in hanging around. As I also told you, I'm not interested in collecting any dues. So far as I'm concerned, you can have it all!'

His jaw tautened abruptly, mouth forming a harder line. 'You think that's all I care about?'

'I think you've probably been groomed to consider yourself the natural successor to all this,' she answered levelly. 'It would only be human nature to resent any possible contender—especially when they're dropped on you the way I've been.'

'It's beyond human nature to do what you're supposedly proposing to do,' came the clipped retort. 'You'd have to be an idiot to take that line, and I reckon you're far from it.'

Gina gazed back at him with a coolness she was far from feeling. 'Idiotic or not, it's the truth.'

'Is this a private fight, or can anyone join in?' asked Elinor Harlow mildly, coming up unnoticed by either of them. 'I must say, for two people who only met a few hours ago, you certainly didn't waste any time getting to grips! Orally, at any rate,' she added with a glimmer of a smile as her son turned a quelling look on her.

She had changed her dress for another in lilac, Gina noted. Not exactly evening wear, but certainly no less dressy than her own. Ross was the odd one out, not her.

Glancing back at him, she caught a derisive gleam in the grey eyes. That he didn't believe a word she'd said was obvious. Well, he'd learn soon enough. Two days maximum, and she was out of here.

He got up to pull out a chair for his mother, sitting down again as drinks arrived borne by a woman in her forties.

'Lydia's our housekeeper,' Elinor said. 'She and Michael take care of everything.'

Michael being the chauffeur, Gina surmised. She smiled at the woman, receiving the briefest acknowledgement. Elinor herself appeared to be the only one ready to offer an unqualified welcome.

'Looking at the two of you, I suppose I should make a bit of an effort,' Ross remarked when Lydia had left. 'Always providing you didn't get round to throwing out my stuff yet?'

Elinor shook her head reprovingly. 'You know perfectly well I haven't.'

'Don't go to any trouble on my account,' Gina told him blandly. 'I've no objection whatsoever to shirtsleeves.'

'I'll bear it in mind.' He drank the rest of his own drink, and pushed back his chair once more. 'See you.'

Elinor eyed Gina shrewdly as her son departed. 'Been getting at you, has he?'

Gina had to smile. 'You could say that. He seems to think I'm lying through my teeth when I say I'm not interested in any financial gain from all this.'

'You have to admit that's an unusual attitude to take,' Elinor commented after a moment. 'Most people in your position would be only too ready to seek compensation.'

'I'm not most people. Naturally, I regret never having known my real mother, but I've had a very good life with two people I love more than anyone in the world. I don't want any compensation.'

'You may have trouble convincing your grandfather of that too,' Elinor said. 'He's full of plans.'

'Then I'm afraid he'll have to unplan.'

The grey eyes, so like her son's, met green for a lengthy

moment, an odd expression in their depths, then she inclined her head. 'You know your own mind.

'Tell me about yourself,' she went on. 'I know you grad-
uated from university, and you have your own business
now, but little else. Is there a man in your life?'

'No one special,' Gina admitted. She adopted a light
note. 'I'm what's known as footloose and fancy-free!'

'Not for lack of offers, I'm sure. You're very lovely.'

Gina gave a laugh. 'By Hollywood standards, I'd
scarcely make first base!'

'You might be pretty shocked if you saw some Hollywood
beauties *au naturel*,' Elinor replied. 'Make-up and lighting
can work miracles. You've no need of enhancement.'

'Thanks.' Gina took it all with a pinch of salt. She'd no
false vanity about her looks, but Elinor was way over the
top. 'Is it always as hot as this?' she asked, more by way
of changing the subject than through any need to know.

'This is cool compared to what it will be in a few weeks,'
Elinor confirmed. 'We get whatever breeze there is up here,
which helps. There's a pool, if you want to cool off any
time. It's down on a lower level. You can't see it from
here. I swim every morning, if you feel like joining me.'

'I'd like to.' Gina could say that much in all honesty.
She liked Elinor Harlow. Better by far than she liked her
son.

She closed her mind to the thought that liking had little
to do with the responses that individual aroused in her.

They talked desultorily for a while, until Ross joined
them again. He was wearing a pair of tailored trousers in
dark blue, along with a white shirt. His thick dark hair was
still damp from the shower, curling a little at the ends.

'Better?' he asked, with a tilt of an eyebrow in Gina's
direction.

'Fine feathers make fine birds,' she responded, adopting the same tone.

'Gina and I were discussing the film industry,' Elinor put in. 'You should take her down to the studio while she's here, Ross. Sam would be only too delighted.'

'According to what she tells me, she isn't going to be here long enough to do any touring,' he said.

'I suppose I could stretch a point,' Gina parried, with absolutely no intention. 'I'm never likely to get the chance to see a film studio again. Of course, if you're too busy...'

He gave a brief shrug. 'I guess I can stretch a point too. I'll make the arrangement. Ready to eat?'

'Well, yes.' She could say that in all honesty. 'Outside or in?'

'Out, but not here. Don't bother bringing your drink,' he added as she made to pick the glass up. 'You can have another.'

'Waste not, want not,' she returned, ignoring the instruction.

Elinor was smiling. 'I think you might have met your match, darling,' she said to her son.

'Don't count on it,' he advised Gina with a challenging glint. 'I'm not on the market.'

'I'm not in the queue,' she returned.

'Let's go and eat,' said Elinor, obviously very entertained by the repartee.

The terrace swept right around the side of the house. Ross saw the two women settled at the table already set out for the meal before taking his own seat. Gina met the grey gaze across the table with an equanimity she was beginning to find a strain to keep up. He disturbed her in more ways than just the one.

The meal was brought out on a heated trolley, from which they all helped themselves. Simply presented though it might be, the food was beautifully prepared. All the same, Gina found herself toying with it, her appetite shrivelled by the tiredness creeping up on her. She'd dozed on the plane, but only fitfully. To all intents and purposes, she'd been up and about for almost twenty-five hours.

'When do I get to meet Roxanne?' she asked at one point, fighting to stay alert.

'When she gets back from Frisco,' Ross supplied. '*If* she gets back before you leave.'

'Stop pushing the girl,' his mother reprimanded. 'She'll leave when she's good and ready to leave.' Her eyes were on Gina's face. 'I think you should go and get a good night's rest. Tomorrow's a new day.'

'You've been reading *Gone with the Wind* again,' commented her son. 'It's time I was off too, if it comes to that. I was due at Pinots an hour ago.'

'I thought the Hollywood scene left you cold,' Elinor remarked.

'Depends who's going to be there.' He was on his feet as he spoke, gaze shifting to Gina. 'I'll let you know about the studio tour.'

'Fine.' She was too tired to conjure any smarter response. 'Goodnight, then.'

'Goodnight.'

She watched him stride across to the house, aware of a spasm deep down inside as she viewed the tapering line from shoulder to hip, the hardness of thigh beneath the fine material of his trousers. It wasn't the first time she'd been physically stirred by a fine male physique, though never quite so strongly, she had to admit.

Forget it, she told herself. The situation was fraught enough without letting sexual attraction in on the act.

'He isn't really as hard as he might appear,' said Elinor,

watching her watching him. 'It's been shock on shock these past weeks.'

'Is there any chance at all for my grandfather?' Gina ventured.

'I'm afraid not. The tumour was inoperable by the time it was diagnosed. You'll find little outward sign of his condition. The medication keeps him pain-free.' Elinor's voice was matter-of-fact, but there was no disguising the pain in her eyes. 'He sent the letter to you before he told us about it. It must have come as a shock for you too.'

'Yes.' The understatement of the year, Gina reflected. 'My parents had no idea of my background.'

'But they didn't object to you coming?'

'Not in the circumstances.' Gina put a hand to her mouth to smother a yawn. 'I'd better call it a day. I can't even think straight right now.'

'Can you find your own way?' Elinor asked. 'Or shall I come with you?'

'I'll be fine.' All Gina wanted at present was to be alone. She gave the older woman a smile. 'See you in the morning, then.'

She went back round the house to enter by the same door from which she'd emerged with Alex a couple of hours or so ago, gaining her room without running into anyone. The bed looked so inviting. She had to force herself to at least remove her make-up before tumbling into it.

Tired though she was, she found sleep hard to come by. Her mind kept endlessly turning. There had never been a shortage of money in the Saxton household. Her father was a company director, her mother the author of two highly acclaimed biographies, their home in Harrow as up-market as any other on the avenue. Far removed from the world these people lived in even so. She may be one of them by birth, but she could never be one of them by choice. Ross was welcome to it all.

# CHAPTER TWO

APART from a certain hesitation in his speech, and some restriction in mobility in his left side, there was, as Elinor had said, little to reveal the ravages the brain tumour was wreaking on Oliver Harlow's body. At sixty-five, he still appeared a fine figure of a man.

'You're Jenny's daughter all right,' he said with a catch in his voice. 'I can't tell you how much it means to me to have you here, Gina. To know I'm forgiven for what I did.'

He was taking a lot for granted, but she let it pass.

'I think the best thing we can both of us do now is put it from mind,' she said. She brightened her voice to add, 'You have a stunning home! I'm only just beginning to find my way around. Your wife and I swam together earlier. Not that I'd have thought the pool needed heating in this climate. You could hard boil an egg in there!!'

Oliver laughed. 'Ross would be the first to agree with you. He refuses to use it himself. Elinor insists on a minimum of eighty. She says anything less is too much of a shock on the system.' He paused, his regard centred on her face. 'How did you and Ross get along yesterday?'

Gina kept her expression bland. 'Like a house on fire. He's quite a character.'

'He's all of that.' There was a note of quiet satisfaction in his voice. 'I recognised his potential even at fourteen. Not entirely my doing, of course, but I like to think I played a major part in shaping him.'

They were seated on the terrace beneath one of the wide

umbrellas. Elinor came to join them, looking from one to the other with quizzically lifted brows.

'So, how are things going?'

'I think we can say things are going very well,' her husband answered. 'You'd agree with that, Gina?'

'Of course.' She could scarcely say anything else, she thought.

'Ross rang a minute or two ago,' Elinor went on. 'He's arranged the studio tour we were talking about last night for this afternoon. The studio head, Sam Walker, is an old family friend.'

'Sam knows Jenny had a baby adopted,' Oliver put in. 'One of the few.'

'To be honest, I'm not all that interested in doing this tour,' Gina admitted.

'If Ross has gone to the trouble of arranging it, you'd better pretend to be,' said her grandfather on a humorous note. 'What time will he be here?'

'In half an hour. He's taking you to lunch first,' Elinor added to Gina. 'He said to tell you not to bother dressing up. You'll be far more comfortable in casual wear.'

Gina kept her tone as free of sarcasm as possible. 'Thoughtful of him to worry about my comfort.' She stirred reluctantly. 'I suppose I'd better go and sort something out, then. I think this...' indicating her brief sun top '...might be just a little *too* casual.'

'With a figure like yours, you could wear a sack and still look good,' Oliver commented with a certain complacency. 'The Harlow women have always been well-structured.'

'He's talking about the boobs, darling,' Elinor advised. 'I'd never have made the grade myself if I'd been flat-chested, would I, honey?'

'Not a chance,' he confirmed.

Seeing the look that passed between the two of them,

Gina felt a sudden pang that could only be envy. Her parents aside, she'd never known that depth of feeling for anyone. How Elinor could joke when she was on the verge of losing the man she so obviously loved to distraction was beyond her.

Back in her room, she surveyed her somewhat scant wardrobe, selecting a pair of cotton jeans in off-white, along with a sleeveless beige sweater. The length of her hair caught back in a tortoiseshell slide, she applied no more than a bare sweep of mascara along her lashes, and a dash of pale pink lipstick. If Ross wanted casual, casual was what he would get.

He was waiting for her in the hall when she went down. He was wearing jeans himself, the cut and fit lifting them into a range of their own. Tucked in at the waist, the cotton T-shirt outlined a well-toned midriff.

'Glad to see you took my advice,' he commented. 'You might find sunglasses a help.'

Gina tapped the small white shoulder-bag she was carrying. 'In here—along with my handkerchief.'

The grin came and went. 'Call it a brotherly concern.'

'Strictly speaking,' she said, 'you'd be an uncle, though I'm sure you'd hate me to call you that.'

'You can count on it.'

There was something different about him this morning, Gina reflected as they made their way outdoors. His mood seemed lighter than yesterday. Perhaps because he'd decided to accept her word that she wanted nothing from this relationship. Truth to tell, she didn't think it was the financial aspect that bothered him so much as the possibility that she might lay claim to the business empire he'd been groomed to take over. Well, he could rest easy on both scores.

The open-topped car parked out on the forecourt was

long and low-slung, its dark blue bodywork gleaming in the sunlight, black leather upholstery masculine as it came. Ross saw her into the front passenger seat before going round to slide behind the wheel.

Gina was vibrantly aware of his proximity. The light covering of hair on the arm he extended to fire the ignition was bleached golden by the sun, causing her to wonder if the hair on his chest—assuming he had hair on his chest—was the same.

Not, she assured herself, that it mattered a damn to her anyway. She couldn't afford to let it matter.

Conversation was kept to a minimum on the drive down. Gina wasn't loath to sit back and just admire the scenery. Beverly Hills. Home to so many famous names both past and present. There was a tour, she recalled reading somewhere, that was supposed to take in the homes belonging to all the major stars. It must be like living in a goldfish bowl!

'The price to be paid,' Ross remarked when she said as much. 'None of them spend all that much time here, anyway, these days.'

'Do you know any of them?'

'One or two. They're people just like you and me.'

Him, maybe, she thought; she was way outside her natural environment.

Anticipating a city venue for lunch, she was taken by surprise when he turned the car in through a wide gateway, only realising that the long, low building in front of them was a hotel when she saw the discreetly displayed sign.

'Is this where you live?' she queried.

Ross indicated the top left-hand corner of the building. 'Right up there. Easier to eat here than get caught up in the mêlée downtown. The restaurants are second to none.'

'You never fancied a home of your own?'

'Too much of a hassle. I travel a lot.'

He brought the car to a stop at the foot of the broad flight of steps leading up to the entrance, getting out to hand over the keys to a young man in a smart green uniform that matched the overhead canopy. Gina slid from her own seat and went to join him as the valet drove the vehicle away.

'Impressive,' she commented, refusing to be overwhelmed. 'And this is only one of…how many?'

'Twenty-three to date. We don't always build, we acquire and rejuvenate. Which one did you sample?'

'New York. A special deal through a friend in a travel agency. Economy each way, plus two nights in the Harlow. Didn't leave much over for a Fifth Avenue shopping spree, but I managed to pick up a few bargains.'

'Worth the trip?'

'Definitely. Jeans like these cost a bomb back home. I only paid forty dollars.'

The appealing grin lit the lean features once more. 'I meant the accommodation.'

Gina kept a straight face. 'As I already told you, very nice. Of course, we were occupying one of the least expensive rooms, and eating out, so we didn't—'

Dark brows lifted quizzically. 'We?'

'I was with a friend.' Her eyes were on the woman who'd just emerged from the hotel. 'That's Shauna Wallis, isn't it?'

'It is,' Ross confirmed. 'She rents a bungalow in the grounds. The friend male or female?'

'Female.' Her attention was still on the star, who had now been joined by a young man wearing tennis whites. 'She looks rather older than I imagined her to be.'

'Natural daylight can be a killer,' Ross rejoined. 'Dennis is our resident pro. He'll be taking her for a session.'

Gina glanced his way appraisingly, registering the slant to his lips. 'You're a cynic,' she accused.

'A realist,' he said. 'Shauna likes fit young men.'

'And you've no objection to a member of staff providing the service?'

'What he gets up to in his lunch hour is his own business. Talking of which, we'd better get to it ourselves if we're to be at the studio for two. Sam's keeping a slot free for us. He knew Jenny, of course. He's looking forward to meeting you.'

Which was more than she could say, Gina reflected wryly, moving on up the steps along with Ross. Something in her shrank from learning too much about the girl who'd given her life—of creating a tie to the past that she might find difficult to sever.

The hotel was superlative, the vast lobby separated into different sitting areas, some upholstered with tropical-style fabrics, others with leather furniture and plenty of marble. Plant life abounded.

There were people sitting around, groups standing chatting, porters trundling trolleys from the long mahogany desk where three receptionists were hard at work, to the bank of elevators.

'Business seems to be good,' Gina commented.

'It always is.' Ross acknowledged a man in a dark grey suit hovering near by. 'We're eating in the Garden Room.'

'Piers has the table ready for you,' the man replied. His glance flickered Gina's way, the speculation obvious. Far from the boss's usual type, she could almost hear him thinking.

The restaurant just off the lobby was crowded, the buzz of conversation loud. Ross didn't bother waiting for attendance, leading the way through to an outdoor section set beneath a vine-covered loggia. Every table but one was occupied out here too. Gina felt the cynosure of all eyes as they took their seats. At least they weren't the only ones dressed casually, she was glad to note.

The *maître d'* came rushing over, looking distinctly put out. 'Never will you allow me to do my job!' he exclaimed.

Ross gave him a dry smile. 'If you're short of something to do, you can fetch me a Moët.'

'Not for me, thanks,' Gina cut in swiftly. 'I don't like champagne. A kir would be fine.'

'Make that two,' Ross ordered. 'I'm driving.'

'You were driving when you asked for champagne,' she pointed out as the man moved off.

'It was meant for you.' His regard was quizzical. 'The first woman I've ever met who doesn't like champagne!'

Her shrug was light. 'So I'm an oddity.'

'A rarity, for sure. Do I order wine?'

'I'd rather keep a clear head.' She toyed with the stem of a glass, unable to relax under his scrutiny. 'Will you stop looking at me as though I just sprouted a second one?'

'I was actually thinking how refreshing it is to entertain a woman of simple tastes,' he said.

'You mix in the wrong circles,' she retorted, by means deaf to satire.

'Difficult to find any other kind in this town. Most are out for the best deal they can manage for themselves. The reason I find your attitude towards money so hard to accept. Oliver would set you up for life.'

Green eyes met grey, holding fast. 'That's not why I'm here, believe me. If my grandfather was fit and well, I wouldn't have come at all.'

'But you couldn't refuse a dying man's plea.'

Faint though it was, the irony set her teeth on edge. It took a real effort to keep her tongue under control. 'That would have been too cruel.'

The arrival of their drinks cut off whatever reply he'd been about to make. He waited until the waiter had gone before saying levelly, 'Oliver won't let you leave empty-handed.'

'I'm afraid he won't have a choice,' she said. 'I like my life the way it is. I don't want it altering.'

'Your business partner might appreciate an extra influx of capital.'

'Barbara doesn't know anything about all this, and isn't going to know. How many times do I have to say it?'

Ross held up a hand. 'All right, I believe you! I think you're crazy, but I believe you.'

'Good.' She took up the leather-bound menu. 'What would you recommend?'

'Try the Colorado lamb,' he suggested. 'It's a house speciality.'

He wasn't exaggerating. Served with a sweet-pepper lasagne, the dish was mouthwateringly enjoyable. Gina refused dessert, settling for coffee. 'You really didn't have to do any of this, you know,' she said, when Ross glanced at his watch. 'Your time must be at a premium.'

'Not to the extent that I can't take the odd day or two out when necessary. You're doing that yourself.' He paused, regard reflective. 'Where does your partner think you are right now?'

'Spain,' she admitted. 'A quick break. Her turn next month.'

'You don't consider her a close enough friend to know the truth?'

'It's a business relationship. There's no reason for her to know.' She stirred restlessly. 'Shouldn't we be going?'

'Sure.' He pushed back his chair to get to his feet, rounding the table before she could move, to help her to hers. 'No check to wait for,' he said. 'One of the fringe benefits.'

There would, Gina imagined, be many. If she was that way inclined, she could no doubt claim free accommodation in any of the Harlow hotels herself.

No point going down that road, she warned, hardening her resolve. Once she left California, the connection would be finished.

They made the studio lot just before two. Beautifully laid-out gardens fronted the series of white bungalows which were the main offices, with the bulk of a dozen or more sound stages looming beyond.

Small and balding, looking anything but the tycoon Gina had expected, Sam Walker was well into his sixties. He had a meeting in ten minutes, he apologised, but they were welcome to tour the lot.

'Jenny was a lovely girl,' he said. 'A bit of a problem at times, maybe, but no worse than many. I've had three of my own, so I know what it's like. You've got the Harlow bones,' he observed judiciously. 'Look good on the screen. I could set up a test.'

Gina laughed, taking the offer no more seriously than she was sure he intended it to be taken. 'I'm no actress.'

He smiled back. 'Few are, honey.' He shifted his gaze to Ross. 'How's Oliver doing?'

Ross lifted his shoulders, face impassive. 'Holding out. I didn't see him this morning.'

'He seemed fine when I left him on the terrace,' Gina said.

'He'd gone back upstairs when I got there. Said he was feeling tired.'

'Hardly surprising,' Sam commented. 'Only wish there was something to be done. Lucky he can rely on you to keep things under control.' He checked the time on a wall clock opposite. 'Afraid that's it for me. You know your way around, Ross. Feel free. I'll call in to see Oliver first chance I get.'

'Will he?' Gina asked when they were outside again. 'Call, I mean.'

'Like he said, when he can fit it in. He's another who finds it hard to delegate.' Ross took her arm as she made to head for the car park across. 'We'll use one of the run-abouts.'

A studio lot, Gina found, was like a city in miniature. It even had its own fire department. There was a whole lake, a waterfront township, mock-ups of city streets. Somewhat disappointingly, there was no outside filming at present, though several of the sound stages were in use.

They were passing one of the latter, when a personnel door set into one of the large rolling ones opened to emit a whole bunch of people. Ross brought the buggy to a stop as a woman detached herself from the centre of the crowd on sight of them, and came over.

'Running tours as a side-line?' she asked. She flicked a swift assessing glance Gina's way. 'Are you going to introduce us, darling?'

'Given half a chance,' Ross said drily. 'Gina Saxton, Karin Trent.'

The woman's striking face and figure and mane of streaked blonde hair were familiar enough for Gina to have already placed the name before Ross spoke. She might have said as much if the other hadn't so obviously dismissed her as of little importance, her attention returned immediately to Ross.

'You'll be in town for the wrap party next week?'

'Doubtful,' he said.

The pout was too little-girly for a mature woman in Gina's eyes. From the way Ross was acting, the interest was one-sided, but it didn't appear to be getting through to her.

'Call me,' she invited.

She didn't stay for an answer, heading back to where her entourage waited, hips swaying seductively as she walked. Ross put the buggy into motion again, face expressionless.

'I saw her in *Captivation* last year,' Gina commented lightly. 'She was good.'

'She can play a part,' he agreed.

'Do you know her intimately?'

He glanced her way, one dark brow lifted. 'Why the interest?'

'I just thought she may have reason to feel a little proprietorial.'

'On the premise that any woman I sleep with has rights?'

Gina kept her tongue tucked firmly in her cheek. 'More than the ones you don't sleep with. You could do a lot worse, anyway. She's very beautiful.'

'No more than a thousand others.'

'Planning on trying them all out?'

He laughed. 'That much stamina I don't have. You needn't concern yourself over Karin. She's a survivor.'

'You're a bit of a bastard at heart, aren't you?' Gina said coolly.

'Only a bit?' Ross sounded more amused than insulted. 'Why start pulling your punches now?'

'I believe in keeping something in reserve.'

She got out from the buggy as he brought it to a halt at the car park, putting up a hand to reposition the tortoiseshell slide, which had started to slip down.

'Why not let it hang loose?' Ross suggested. 'You have beautiful hair.'

'It's out of the way,' she said, unable to deny a stirring of pleasure at the compliment. 'I'm not out to make an

'I didn't think you'd be in today, Mr Harlow!' she exclaimed.

'A brief visit,' he assured her. 'I need to check a couple of details.'

Corridors led off to either hand. He chose the right, opening the first door to reveal a huge office with a magnificent view out over the city to the Santa Monica mountains. The desk was a solid block of black mahogany, set at right angles to another holding a communications complex. A group of soft leather club chairs were arranged about a low square coffee-table to form a relaxed conversation area. The same thick cream carpeting was run through here too.

'Have a seat,' Ross invited. 'This won't take long.'

Gina took one of the upright ones set close by the desk as he went behind it to slide into the big leather executive chair. A press of a button brought a computer screen to humming life.

'Everything at the fingertips,' she commented, watching him scroll down a file menu. 'What did we do before computers were invented?'

'Relied even more on a good secretary,' he said. 'Penny's still indispensable.'

'She's very attractive.'

'Isn't she though?' His eyes were still on the screen. 'Happily married, in case you're wondering. And…'

He broke off at the sound of a phone, extracting a mobile from a pocket. 'Harlow,' he announced. 'Oh, hi! What…?' He broke off again, face tautening as he listened. 'We'll be there ASAP.'

Already alerted, Gina came to her feet along with him. 'What is it?'

'Oliver,' he said tersely. 'He had a heart attack. They're on the way to hospital.'

As they battled the late-afternoon traffic build-up, the

journey back across the city was a nightmare. Gina sat through it numbly. She had spent no more than half an hour with her grandfather this morning: there was a very real possibility that it might be the only time she was ever going to have with him.

Ross was silent throughout, but the taut set of his jaw spoke volumes. There was no doubting his feelings for the man who had taken the place of his own father.

They reached the hospital at last, to be directed straight to the coronary unit. They found Elinor seated in a plush waiting room, with a nurse in attendance. The face she raised to her son was tragic.

'He's gone,' she said.

# CHAPTER THREE

THE funeral service was attended by what seemed to Gina to be half the city. No more than thirty were invited back to the house afterwards, though several more took it on themselves to make the journey.

Pale but composed, Elinor moved among them, accepting the sympathetic offerings with a word of gratitude, smiling at the anecdotes. Gina admired her fortitude.

It had been taken for granted that she would stay on. Not that she could have brought herself to leave in such circumstances anyway. She'd been forced to tell Barbara the truth, and knew she was going to have some explaining to do when she did get back.

Ross caught her eye, his smile reassuring. He'd been a tower of strength these past few days, making all the arrangements, contacting the necessary people. He'd had trouble locating his sister. Gina had stood in for her when Elinor had so desperately needed another woman to talk to. Not that Roxanne had appreciated it.

Talking animatedly with Sam Walker at present, she showed little sign of grief. The black suit sat her tall, willowy figure beautifully, the whiteness of the silk shirt worn beneath contrasting with the darkness of her hair. She had good looks in abundance, marred only, in Gina's estimation, by a certain hardness about her mouth.

She had made her views clear the moment the two of them met. Not in actual words at the time, but the look in her eyes had left little unsaid. Later, when they were alone, she had left no doubt at all of her feelings. The adoption ruled out any claim on the estate, she declared. Considering her unchanged intentions, Gina hadn't bothered arguing the point.

Ross brought a glass of what looked like whisky across. 'Drink this,' he commanded. 'You look as if you need a stimulant.'

What she needed, she thought, was a good dose of home. Failing that, the whisky would have to do. She took the glass from him and swallowed half the contents in one go, grimacing as the spirit hit the back of her throat.

'Steady,' he warned. 'That's neat Rye.'

'Now he tells me!' Her eyes sought his, knowing she would read nothing there that he didn't want her to see. 'Your mother is bearing up well.'

'She'll make it through. Another half an hour, then I'll start clearing this lot out.' He studied her reflectively. 'Thanks for giving her so much support.'

'No problem,' Gina assured him. 'I only wish there was more I could do. I know how much she loved Oliver.'

'It's going to hit her even harder tonight when it's all over. I'll be staying on.'

'Good.' Gina was relieved to know she wouldn't be facing a lone session with Roxanne should Elinor retire early. 'Tomorrow should be a little easier.'

Ross shook his head. 'Not really. There's the will-reading.'

'Is that absolutely necessary?' she asked. 'I'd have thought it was pretty straightforward.'

'The main part, maybe. But there'll be other bequests. It's a formality that has to be gone through.'

One that could surely wait a while, Gina thought, but what did she know?

'I'd better make some arrangements myself tomorrow,' she said.

Something flickered in the grey eyes. 'Of course. I'll be contacting your parents to thank them for the flowers. That was a nice gesture.'

Sam Walker detached himself from the small group now formed about Roxanne, and came over. He acknowledged Gina with a faint smile and a comforting pat on the arm before turning to Ross.

'Afraid I'll have to get moving,' he said gruffly.

Ross grasped the hand held out to him. 'Thanks for coming, Sam. It can't have been easy.'

The shrug was brief. 'What is? I'll catch your mother on the way out. Keep in touch.'

'He lost his wife last year,' Ross explained as the older man wended his way through the throng. 'As Hollywood marriages go, theirs was one of the rare exceptions.'

'You don't think he'll ever marry again?' Gina murmured.

'Doubtful. Although there are plenty would be more than willing.'

Gina could imagine. The head of a leading studio would be some catch! She felt a sudden wave of self-disgust; she was turning into a real cynic herself. The sooner she was on that plane heading homewards, the better.

'I owe you an apology,' said Ross unexpectedly. 'I was pretty rotten to you when you first arrived.'

Green eyes met grey, striving to conceal her inner emotions. 'Nothing I couldn't handle.'

'So I discovered. I doubt if anything could faze you.'

He didn't know the half of it, she thought. 'I try not to let it,' she returned. 'Shouldn't you be circulating?'

'I've spoken with everyone I need to. Some of them are here uninvited anyway.' He indicated an unoccupied sofa near by. 'Why don't we sit down for a few minutes? It's been a long day.'

Gina couldn't argue with that. She felt bone weary. Ross seized two cups of coffee from the trolley being wheeled around the assembly, depositing them on the low table in front of the sofa to take a seat alongside her.

'Better,' he said.

'Much,' Gina agreed. 'A good thing you decided to hold this inside. The heat out there would have been too much.' She viewed the spacious, luxuriously furnished living room. 'Do you think your mother will stay on here?'

'It's a question I've already asked myself,' he said. 'She'd be better off taking an apartment, where she'd be among people. Whether she'll be ready to do that is something else. She and Oliver spent the whole of their married life together in this house. Not the same one he shared with your grandmother,' he added.

Gina cast an oblique glance at him as he lifted the coffee-cup to his lips, devouring the clean lines of his body in the black suit, the strongly defined contours of his face.

'Does Roxanne always stay here when she's in town?' she asked, needing some distraction.

'When it suits.' There was a sudden harder note to his voice. 'Roxanne does what's best for Roxanne.'

'That doesn't sound very brotherly.'

'Siblings aren't always compatible. We live very different lives. The odds against the two of you getting on were pretty high.'

Gina shot him another glance. 'Why do you say that?'

'Ideals. You have them, Roxanne doesn't. None that I've gleaned, anyway.'

People were beginning to show signs of leaving. He put the cup down and got to his feet again. 'I'd better go and do the honours.'

Gina retired to the terrace until it was over, taking stock of what he'd said about his sister. It had come as something

of a shock, she had to admit. Whatever her own opinion of
the woman, she would have anticipated a very different
attitude from him. It was almost as though he despised her.

Something radical had to have happened between the two
of them to cause such a reaction. Not that she was ever
likely to find out; she wasn't even sure she'd want to. In a
day or two she'd be gone, and could put the whole thing
behind her.

It wasn't going to be that easy, she knew. Ross had made
too much of an impression to be cast from mind. She'd
known the first moment she set eyes on him that it was
going to be like that. It happened sometimes; she'd just
never expected it to happen to her.

One thing she was pretty certain of: while he'd mellowed
towards her on a general front, that was as far as it went
for him. No surprise there. She had nothing at all in common with the kind of women he was accustomed to.

Elinor had apparently retired from the fray when she
made her way back indoors again, leaving Ross to deal with
the remaining stragglers. A glass still in hand, Roxanne
viewed her with open contempt.

'There's nothing for you to hang around for now,' she
said. 'Why not book yourself a flight home?'

'I intend to,' Gina told her levelly. 'First thing in the
morning.'

'What's wrong with tonight?'

'I'm tired.'

'You mean you're hoping my mother is going to beg
you to stay on!' The striking face was hard set. 'Don't think
I'm blind to the way you've been sucking up to her!'

'I've been doing the job you should have been doing,'
Gina retorted bitingly, unable to hold back under the on-
slaught. 'Trying to offer some comfort.'

'I don't need you to tell me how to act,' came the scathing reply.

'Somebody should.'

'What's going on?' asked Ross, approaching unnoticed by either of them. He looked from one to the other, brows lifted. 'So?'

'I suggested it was time she thought about going home, that's all,' said his sister.

'It's up to Gina to decide for herself,' he stated flatly. 'You could say she's more right to be here than any of us.'

'That's garbage!'

'It's immaterial,' Gina put in firmly before Ross could answer. 'Anyway, I'm going up to change.'

'Good idea,' he said. 'Oliver would probably have disapproved of the black to start with. He always thought the Irish had the right idea when it came to funerals.' He eyed his sister, expression hardening. 'Are you planning on staying?'

'I'm not planning on going anywhere until I know how I stand,' she retorted.

'Now, why would I think otherwise?'

Gina left them to it. Whatever the source of their alienation, it wasn't her business. Gaining the privacy of her room, she stood for a moment or two to collect herself. It was already coming up to six o'clock, which meant they'd been on the go for almost eleven hours. A well-organised eleven hours, perhaps, but no less draining. Elinor must be feeling totally done in.

It was going to be hard leaving her too. They'd become close over the past days. Elinor hadn't said a word against her daughter, though the latter's neglect must have hurt. Roxanne was only interested in what was good for Roxanne, Ross had said. She could believe it.

A needle-like cold shower went some way towards a

physical refreshment. The lounging trousers and matching loose top she donned had been worn before, but her wardrobe had been meant to see her over two or three days at the most, not a week or more. The dress she'd worn that day was the one she'd worn that first evening here, with a silky black jacket concealing the low-cut neckline. She could have bought more clothes, of course, only what would have been the point?

She found Ross on his own downstairs. He'd changed from the black suit into cream trousers and shirt.

'Drink?' he asked.

'Just orange juice, please,' she said.

'Still keeping a clear head?'

'Still recovering from the whisky you gave me,' she countered. 'Is your mother coming down?'

'Shortly.' He brought the glass across. 'Roxanne won't be joining us. She decided there were far more entertaining places to be downtown.'

'Has she always been like that?' Gina asked after a moment.

'Self-centred?' He lifted his shoulders. 'As far back as I can remember. Having Oliver as a father did her no good at all. He was so anxious for her to accept him, he indulged her every whim.'

'Did he indulge you too?'

'He didn't need to. We hit it off from the start. He'd always wanted a son. Maybe if you'd been a boy…' He left it there with another brief shrug. 'We'll never know, will we?'

There was a pause before he spoke again, his regard steady. 'You've been a godsend this last week. Don't think it isn't appreciated.'

'I did nothing special,' she protested.

'You were there for my mother when she needed the

kind of support only another woman can provide. You encouraged her to let it all out instead of bottling it up the way she probably would have done. If Roxanne...' He broke off again, shaking his head. 'What's the point?'

Gina bit back the question trembling on the tip of her tongue. Her involvement with this family was over. It *had* to be over.

She had to keep reminding herself of that throughout the evening. Pale but composed, Elinor accepted her daughter's absence with a wry expression that made Gina seethe at the latter's total lack of filial feeling. None of them ate a great deal, and she was unsurprised when Elinor retired almost immediately after the meal.

'I think I might have an early night myself,' she said into the silence that followed her departure.

'Stay a while,' Ross requested softly. 'I don't feel like being on my own.'

Meeting the grey eyes, Gina subsided back into her seat. 'It must have been hard,' she said, 'to keep up the front all week.'

His smile was faint. 'Pretty hard, yes.'

'I never could understand why men feel they have to keep their emotions under wraps.'

'Childhood conditioning.' There was a pause, a change of tone. 'What was your initial reaction when you got Oliver's letter?'

'Disbelief,' she acknowledged. 'I was sure there must be some mistake.'

'It made no difference to your feelings for the Saxtons?'

'Of course not. There's more to parenthood than just giving birth. They've been wonderful parents.'

'Are they in a position to help you buy your way out of this partnership?'

Brought up short, Gina took a moment or two to gain a

hold on herself. 'What makes you think I want out?' she demanded.

Ross lifted his shoulders. 'Instinct. You're unwilling to talk about the business, and you obviously don't have much of a regard for your partner outside of it.'

'That's very little to go on.'

'But you can't deny it.'

Green eyes flared, the anger overtaken almost immediately by wry acknowledgement as they held the steady grey gaze. 'All right, I can't deny it. And yes, I suppose they would be in a position, if I were willing to ask them. It was my mistake. I'll deal with it.'

'You're a one-off, do you know that?' he said softly. 'In this part of the world, at any rate.'

Gina felt her pulse rate shoot into overdrive as he got to his feet and came over to where she sat. She made no protest when he drew her from the chair, going into his arms without thought of anything beyond this moment.

His mouth was gentle at first, seeking rather than demanding, hardening to passion by slow degrees as the response built in her. It was what she had wanted all week: what she had wanted since the moment she set eyes on him, if she was honest about it. Nothing else mattered right now but the need he was arousing in her, the overwhelming desire to be closer still. He felt the same way, that was obvious. For the moment, at any rate.

She had a brief moment of sanity on the way to her room, but it didn't last. The feel of him at her side, the hand so strong and firm on hers, the subtle masculine scent of him, were enough to drive all other considerations into oblivion.

They undressed each other between kisses, scattering garments behind them as they moved inexorably towards the bed. Ross stood for a moment to view her as she lay nude on the silken cover, eyes travelling the length of her slender curves.

'You're beautiful,' he breathed.

Magnificent, was the adjective that sprang to her mind as she studied him in turn. His body was honed to a peak of fitness, chest broad and deep, narrowing down to waist and hip, the muscle ribbed across his stomach. The wiry curls of hair covering his chest were marginally lighter in colour than those enclosing the essence of his manhood.

He lay down at her side on the bed, propping himself on an elbow to watch her face as he drifted a fingertip down between her breasts and over the fluttering plane of her stomach with exquisite sensitivity. Gina felt the spasms start deep, her thighs parting of their own accord to allow him free access to the moist centre he sought.

She was ready for him now, but he was in no hurry to seek release for himself, making her writhe and arch in a mixture of agony and ecstasy—drawing moan after moan from her throat as he took all control away from her.

'Enough!' she heard herself pleading. 'No more!'

Ross gave a low laugh. 'We didn't even get started yet!'

He lowered his head to take one peaking, aching nipple between lips and teeth in a combination of nibbling and sucking that drove her wild. She ran her fingers into the thick dark hair, relishing the clean crisp feel of it—holding him close even as she begged him to stop.

By the time he finally moved on top of her, she was almost over the top herself. The sensation when he slid inside her was like nothing she had ever known. Even then, he kept control of himself, his movements measured, deepening the penetration by slow degrees until he reached a point where he couldn't hold out any longer himself.

It was some time before either of them could find the

strength to move so much as a limb. Gina had never felt so totally enervated in her life.

'Well worth waiting for,' Ross murmured against her shoulder.

'Waiting for?' she queried hazily.

'I could have done that the very first night you were here,' he said.

Gina was silent for a moment or two, absorbing the claim. 'You didn't give that impression,' she said at length.

He gave the same low laugh, putting his lips to the side of her neck just below her ear. 'I didn't intend to.'

'Because you believed I was only here for what I could get?'

'Something like that. There's a hell of a difference between lust and trust.'

'But you trust me now?'

'After the way you've acted these past few days, I can't do anything else,' he said softly. 'Mother would have gone to pieces without you.'

'She'd have had you.'

'I couldn't have provided the kind of support you provided. I already told you that.'

He kissed her again, on the lips this time, bringing her back to life. Gina thrust the thoughts hovering on the edge of her mind aside as desire rose in her once more. Whatever the consequences, she was way past saying no to this.

The sun was well up in the sky when she woke from a sleep that had held a quality of exhaustion. Ross was gone from her side, of course. She would have expected nothing else.

Last night had been a serious mistake; she'd known it even while it was happening. Leaving was going to be so much harder.

Not that it would make a great deal of difference to Ross, she was sure. He'd needed a woman last night, and she had been available. He'd even been prepared, she recalled, which suggested forward planning. The pleasure he'd so obviously gained from making love to her would be no more than he was accustomed to gaining from any woman for certain.

Neither Ross nor his sister were about when she went down. She settled for coffee and toast for breakfast, then took the opportunity to make a phone call before going to look for Elinor. She found her laid out on the pool deck.

'Why not join me?' the other invited. 'It's going to rain later.'

'I have to pack,' Gina told her. 'I rang the airport. I'm on a flight at ten-fifteen tonight.'

Elinor sat up abruptly. 'You can't go yet. There's Oliver's will to be read. I told you he'd made plans.'

Gina sank to a seat on a nearby lounger. It had been inevitable from the start, she supposed. 'I really wish he hadn't,' she said. 'It wasn't why I came.'

'I know that. I told Oliver how you felt.' Elinor shook her head. 'It made no difference. I didn't really expect it to. The will was redrawn to include you before you got here. He didn't tell me exactly what he intended, but I'm sure you'll find yourself well able to travel first class from now on. If you try turning it down,' she added, 'it will be like kicking him in the face.'

Gina bit her lip. 'That puts me in a cleft stick.'

'So, accept it.' Elinor gave a faint smile. 'Is money such an evil thing?'

'No,' Gina was bound to admit. 'I just didn't...'

'Didn't want any of us seeing you as a gold-digger,' Elinor finished for her as her voice petered out. 'Oliver made sure you were a worthy bearer of the Harlow blood-

line before he wrote you that letter, believe me. The fact
that you looked for nothing from him only served to prove
he'd made no mistake about you. Ross had his doubts to
begin with, but you've even managed to win him over.'

'But not Roxanne,' Gina said, shying away from thinking
about Ross right now.

Elinor gave a sigh. 'I'm afraid Roxanne sees you as a
threat to the size of her own inheritance. Not that Oliver
will have left her anything but well provided for. Ross will
be taking control of the company, of course. Oliver always
intended he should. The reason he insisted on a legal adoption, so that the name at least would be continued. I was
unable to have any more children myself,' she went on,
sensing the unspoken question. 'Oliver knew that when he
married me. What he did to Jenny and you was wrong—
no one can ever deny that—but he was a good man in so
many other ways.'

'I'm sure of it.' Gina's voice was gentle. 'He obviously
loved you a great deal.'

Tears glistened momentarily in the older woman's eyes.
'I loved him a great deal too. Which is why I'd move
heaven and earth to see his wishes fulfilled.'

Leaving her with very little choice, Gina acknowledged.
'All right,' she said resignedly. 'What time will the reading
be?'

'Two o'clock.'

'Then there's no reason why I can't make that flight.'

'I'd really appreciate it if you could stay a little longer,'
Elinor entreated. 'You're the only one I can talk to. Your
partner can surely handle the business for a few more
days?'

Another cleft stick, Gina thought unhappily. If she insisted on leaving, she let Elinor down, yet if she stayed on,
Ross might take it that she'd read more into last night than

he'd ever intended. Her acceptance of whatever her grandfather had left her was going to prove embarrassing enough
after all her protestations, without that.

'I imagine so,' she said, without allowing herself any
more time to think about it. 'I'll give her a call.'

She left Elinor to resume her sunbathing, and went back
indoors. There was a telephone in her room, but she
couldn't summon the energy to go all the way up there. It
would be well into the afternoon back home, she calculated,
though Barbara should still be at the shop.

She was. What she wasn't was delighted to hear what
her partner had to say.

'It's already been more than a week,' she complained.
'How *much* longer?'

'Two or three days,' Gina hazarded. 'I'm sure you're
managing just fine without me. Anyway, I'll be in touch as
soon as I have a return date.'

Roxanne was standing a few feet away when she turned
from the hall phone. From the way she was dressed, Gina
could only deduce that she'd only just returned from last
night's outing.

'Had a good time?' she asked before the other could
speak.

'Very, if it's any concern of yours,' came the taut reply.
'If you think you're staying on here, you can think again!'

'Would that really be any concern of *yours*?' Gina returned levelly. 'I was under the impression that this is your
mother's house.'

Eyes glittering, Roxanne looked ready to spit. Gina left
her standing there. Not for the first time, she wished none
of this had ever happened; that her grandfather had just let
the past ride. His attack of conscience had turned her life
upside down in more ways than just the one.

She made no mention of the will when she phoned her

parents later. There was little point until she knew what she would be dealing with. They did their best to empathise with Elinor's needs in the circumstances, but it was apparent that they were none too happy. It couldn't be easy for them, Gina reflected wryly.

The morning wore on. Neither brother nor sister put in an appearance for lunch.

'Ross went in to the office,' Elinor said. 'Roxanne is probably still sleeping off last night's excesses.' She sighed and shook her head. 'I really don't know how she got to be the way she is these days. She's my daughter, and I love her, of course, but there are times when I really don't like her very much.'

She said no more, looking as though she regretted having said as much as she had. Gina wished she could offer some reassurance, but she'd have to lie through her teeth to do it. Roxanne was a spoilt bitch; there were no other words for her.

Ross arrived some minutes after the lawyer who was to perform the will-reading, joining the gathering in the library with apologies for keeping them all waiting. Gina kept her eyes fixed firmly to the front as he took a seat close by, but she was conscious of his gaze. So much for all the denials, she could sense him thinking.

The lawyer dealt first of all with the more minor bequests, including the staff. They were then asked to leave the room while the rest of the will was read. Listening to the seemingly endless list of charities and organisations deemed worthy of benefit, Gina could only assume that the sums being tossed around were of little overall importance.

She heard Roxanne mutter, 'About time too!' when they finally came to the main bequests.

'To my adopted daughter, Roxanne,' the lawyer read out,

'I leave the sum of one million dollars, invested to provide an income for life. To my beloved wife, Elinor, I leave—'

'A lousy million!' Roxanne was on her feet, eyes blazing. 'He can't do this to me!'

'Shut up, and sit down!' said Ross forcefully. 'Be thankful he didn't cut you out altogether. One more word, and you're out of here,' he threatened as she opened her mouth to loose another tirade.

'To my beloved wife, Elinor,' the lawyer repeated as Roxanne subsided reluctantly, 'I leave all my worldly goods and personal finances.'

He paused, as if gathering himself, not lifting his eyes from the page in front of him. 'My company holdings I leave to be equally divided between my adopted son, Ross Harlow, and my granddaughter, Virginia Saxton, on condition that the two of them marry. Should they fail to comply with said condition, the shares to be thrown open to the rest of the board.'

# CHAPTER FOUR

THE silence that reigned after that final announcement seemed to last for ever. Gina felt as if she'd been hit over the head with a brick.

Roxanne was the first to recover the power of speech. 'There's no way I'm standing for this!' she jerked out. 'I get a lousy million while *she* gets half the company! Ross, don't just sit there!'

'What would you have me do?' he asked on what Gina considered an astonishingly calm note.

'We can contest it. He wasn't in his right mind!'

'Don't you dare say that!' Elinor flared. 'Oliver knew what he was doing. Gina has Harlow blood in her veins. She has a right to inherit!'

Gina found her voice with an effort, forcing herself to look directly at Ross. 'I'd no idea this was going to happen. I didn't even know I was in the will at all until your mother told me this morning.'

'That was all I knew myself,' Elinor declared. 'Oliver didn't tell me what his intentions were. Not that I find it so unreasonable,' she added staunchly.

Roxanne gazed at her incredulously. 'Are *you* mad too?'

'Don't speak to her like that!' Ross clipped. 'It's obvious that Oliver was going to make provision for his grand-daughter. Admittedly, I didn't anticipate he'd go quite this far, but I'm sure we can sort something out.'

Such as what? Gina wondered, still too dazed to think straight. How could her grandfather have done this to the

51

man he'd groomed to take over from him? How could he have done it to her, if it came to that?

Ross looked across at her, his expression controlled. 'I think we need to talk. Not here. Alone.'

A part of her wanted to say here and now that there was no point in discussing something that wasn't going to happen, but some instinct kept the words from forming. She got to her feet like an automaton to accompany him from the room. Raised once more in bitter complaint, Roxanne's voice was a chain-saw in her ears.

Ross took her to what had been her grandfather's study, inviting her to a seat. He didn't sit down himself, leaning against the desk edge with hands thrust deep into trouser pockets. Looking at him now, Gina found it hard to believe that last night had ever happened.

'I don't...' she began, breaking off as Ross shook his head.

'You don't have to convince me. You were as shocked as any of us back there. I've no quarrel with Oliver's sentiments, only with his manner of expressing them. I think the tumour must have affected his reasoning. Otherwise, he'd have seen how impossible a situation he was creating. However, what's done is done. Short of contesting the will in court—which I've no intention of doing—we're left with two options.'

He held up a staying hand as she made to speak. 'Hear me out. I have a fifteen-per-cent holding, Oliver had sixty, with the other twenty-five spread across the board. If we don't comply with the condition he set down, we'll be giving certain members the opportunity to acquire enough stock to take over control of the company. I've no intention of allowing that to happen either.' The pause was brief. 'Which reduces the options to just the one.'

Gina gazed at him in silence for several moments,

searching the lean features for some sign of the man she'd spent the night with. There was no softening of expression as he gazed back at her—no penetrating the grey eyes. He was a totally unknown quantity again.

'In your view, perhaps,' she got out. 'Not in mine! You really think I'd marry a man I don't even know just to...' She broke off as he tilted an ironic eyebrow, feeling the warmth rising under her skin. 'Just to satisfy his lust for power!' she finished on a hardened edge.

'It won't be just to my advantage,' he returned imperturbably. 'You'll be worth millions in your own right. Can you honestly say that means nothing at all to you?'

She could say it, Gina acknowledged wryly, but it wouldn't be true. Who could possibly be unaffected by the idea of being worth millions?

'No, I can't,' she admitted. 'But money isn't the be-all and end-all. There's such a thing as integrity.'

'You think Oliver was lacking it in making the condition to start with?'

'I think you were right about his judgement being affected,' she said carefully.

Ross studied her for a lengthy moment or two, still giving little away. When he spoke again it was with a certain calculation.

'It won't be a long-term marriage. There's nothing to stop us divorcing after everything is settled. In the meantime, we both live our own lives. I'd continue to run the company, of course. You needn't be involved. All I'd ask is that you sell me enough shares to make up the fifty-one per cent for overall control.'

The anger flooding her had all the force of a rip tide. Last night had meant nothing to him because she meant nothing to him. She'd known that, of course, but having it rammed down her throat this way was too much! The urge to get back at him overrode all other considerations, bringing unstudied words to her lips.

'I might not have your business acumen, but if I go along with this I'll be taking my place on the board—both before and after the divorce.'

'Don't be ridiculous!' Ross's jaw was hard set. 'You've about as much idea of running a company as I have of stocking a boutique!'

'So, you'll just have to show me the ropes. You'll still be the major stock-holder.'

The grey eyes were like granite. 'I thought I had you figured. Seems I was wrong.'

'All the way,' she retorted, still carried along on the same furious wave. 'I won't pretend last night wasn't enjoyable, but don't run away with the idea that it affects here and now in any way. As your mother pointed out, I'm the only real Harlow. Not that I object to you having top billing. My grandfather regarded you highly.'

The curl of his lip had the same impact as a slap in the face, jolting her to her senses for a moment. But only for a moment. She'd chosen her path, she told herself doggedly; she wasn't going to detour from it now. What kind of an idiot would she be to turn her back on millions?

'I guess the boutique's no longer an issue,' he said.

Gina lifted her shoulders. 'Barbara can have it and be welcome.'

'And your parents? How are they likely to react?'

Up until this moment, she hadn't given a thought to that aspect. But she'd gone too far now to turn back.

'They'll cope,' she said, shocked by how callous she sounded. 'They'd want what's best for me.'

Ross gave a brief, grim smile. 'Fair enough. We'll start in the morning. There's a board meeting scheduled at ten.'

It was going too fast. Far too fast! Yet something in her

refused to let go. 'I'll look forward to it,' she said. 'Shall we be going in together?'

'Michael will bring you in. I shan't be here in the morning.'

'Someone else scheduled for tonight?' she asked sweetly. 'Karin Trent, maybe? She certainly seemed eager enough.'

Ross didn't rise to it. 'We'd better go and tell the others what's happening. You'll find Roxanne a lot harder to deal with than my mother, but don't look to me for help.'

'I shan't need any help,' she declared with more spirit than conviction. 'Your sister's claws aren't *that* sharp.'

One dark brow lifted sardonically. 'I wouldn't count on it.'

Gina got to her feet, not in the least surprised to feel her legs give. She stiffened as he moved instinctively to slide a steadying hand beneath her elbow, jerking away from him. 'I'm fine!'

Ross made no answer. He looked totally in command of himself again. She hardened her resolve, refusing to listen to the small inner voice warning of heartache to come from all this.

They found Elinor and Roxanne in the living room. His job done for now, the lawyer had departed.

'If you think I'm settling for a lousy million, you're mistaken!' Roxanne burst out the moment they appeared. 'I want what's due to me!'

'You're getting a great deal more than you merit,' her brother answered shortly. 'If it had been up to me, you'd have got nothing.'

'You're so damned self-righteous!' she flung at him. 'There are two sides to every tale!'

'I've heard your side,' he said. 'Countless times! Anyway, it isn't you we're here to discuss.' He shifted his glance to his mother. 'We're going through with it.'

Totally disregarding the circumstances, Elinor looked frankly delighted. She came over to give Gina a hug. 'There's no one I'd rather have for a daughter-in-law!'

Gina swallowed thickly, wondering if she'd be quite so enthusiastic if she knew how short a duration the relationship would have. The deeper she got into this charade, the worse it became. It wasn't too late to back out, of course. All she had to do was say the word.

'I assume you'll want the wedding as soon as possible,' Elinor said, addressing her son. 'We might just about manage it in a month with the right people organising.'

'Don't get carried away,' he returned drily. 'A civil ceremony will be quite adequate.'

'You can't do that!' She sounded horrified. 'Not for *this* family in *this* town! It has to be the full works!'

'I don't think so.'

'I do.' Gina said it with deliberation, anger at his summary dismissal overruling any wavering. 'Your mother's right. It will be expected.'

Ross slanted a lip. 'If you fancy being the centre of a media circus, by all means go ahead. Just don't complain when your whole life story is put under the microscope!'

'It's all going to come out anyway,' Elinor declared. 'A quiet wedding isn't going to stop the circus. The best way of handling it all is to carry on regardless.'

She turned her attention back to Gina, her smile reassuring. 'You'll stay here for the time being, of course. Michael can drive you around until you get a car. Or there's Oliver's Cadillac in the garage still. I know he'd have wanted you to have it.'

'I think I'd as soon wait until I know my way around a little better,' Gina responded, feeling everything starting to spin out of control again. 'It's such a huge city.'

'Afraid of getting lost?' Roxanne sneered.

Gina didn't turn her head. 'I think that's what I just said, yes. I'll study a map before I venture out on my own.'

'I need a drink,' Ross said brusquely. 'Anyone else?'

'Too early for me,' declared Elinor.

It was still only a little gone three, Gina realised with a sense of shock, glancing at her watch.

'I'll have a gin and tonic, please,' she said, in need of a rod to stiffen her backbone.

Roxanne stalked across to the door, her face set in hard, ugly lines. It will stay like that if the wind changes, Gina was tempted to comment, refraining on the grounds that it was scarcely an adult way to behave. Roxanne had been her enemy since the moment they'd met. Understandably, she was even further from mellowing now.

It was impossible to restrain her curiosity over what she could have done to turn her brother so much against her. Oliver too, if the comparatively paltry sum he had left her was anything to go by. From the way the will had been worded, she wouldn't even be able to get her hands on the capital.

Not her concern, anyway. She was going to have enough on her plate living up to the role she had landed herself in.

She watched Ross as he poured the drinks, unable to conquer the quivering deep down in the pit of her stomach at the images impressed on her mind's eye of that leanly muscled masculine body devoid of all clothing. When it came to performance in bed, he knew it all. Born of experience, of course. He'd probably lost count of the number of women he'd had.

Married, they'd each live their own lives, he'd said in the study. That meant they'd both of them be free to do whatever they wanted to do. For him, that would definitely include seeing other women.

There was no mistaking the emotion running through her

at the thought. While he might not be quite the man she had thought him to be, he still had the same hold on her. A major part of the reason she had agreed to comply with the condition, if she was honest about it—for what good it would do her. He'd wanted her last night, and might well want her again if she showed willing, but it wouldn't mean anything. This was to be a marriage of convenience, nothing more.

She steeled herself to meet his eyes when she took the glass from him, to thank him for it levelly. As usual, she had no idea what was going on in his mind.

'You're going to need to extend your wardrobe, of course,' Elinor announced. 'I can meet you downtown for lunch tomorrow, then show you the best places to go.'

'She might prefer to have her own things sent over,' Ross observed.

'I'm talking about now,' his mother returned. She looked animated, her eyes sparkling the way they hadn't done in days. 'You'll be expected to attend all kinds of functions, Gina. There's a big charity event coming up. You'll need something really special for that.'

'You'll scare the girl to death,' Ross commented drily.

If Gina had been beginning to feel a bit overwhelmed, the "girl" gave her the impetus to rise above it. 'On the contrary,' she said coolly, 'I can't wait to get started. It's a great idea, Elinor. The clothes I have back home wouldn't be suitable anyway.'

Ross shrugged. 'Fine. I'll make sure you have the backing. It's going to take a day or two to get accounts opened for you.'

'I can cover my own expenses!' Gina flashed, evoking another of the sardonic smiles.

'The places my mother will have in mind, I'd doubt it.'

'He's right,' Elinor agreed. 'A dress suitable for the

event I'm talking about will cost several thousand dollars alone, to say nothing of the rest. In the circles you'll be moving in, the clothes say it all.'

Gina bit her lip, only just beginning to realise what she had let herself in for. 'It seems I don't have much choice, then,' she said.

'Wonderful! We'll go to Harry's Bar for lunch, then hit Rodeo. The little cream suit you had on the other day will be quite suitable.' She gave a laugh. 'No pun intended!'

It was worth a great deal to see her mood so much lightened, Gina reflected, smiling with her. She sobered again inwardly on remembering that while Elinor could hardly imagine the marriage was an ideal love match, she had no notion that it would only be a temporary one. Now wasn't the time to disillusion her though.

Ross left half an hour later without attempting any further one-to-one commune. Gina had a feeling he was relying on tomorrow's meeting to show her just how ridiculous her aims in that direction at least were. In truth, she had to agree with him, but she wasn't prepared to let him push her aside. What she didn't know, she could learn.

Elinor filled in a little more detail about the company for her. Oliver had handed over the presidential reins to Ross when he was diagnosed. Including herself, the board now totalled nine. Four members, led by a man called Warren Boxhall, were keen to see the company floated on the open market. A move Oliver had rejected out of hand, as had Ross.

'As there's no chance now of Warren buying up enough stock to gain control, he'll try to persuade you into seeing things his way,' Elinor warned. 'With your thirty per cent alongside, they could force the issue.'

'So far as I'm concerned, the company is totally safe,' Gina assured her.

Elinor smiled. 'I'm sure of it. You're a Harlow through and through.' She hesitated before adding. 'I know this marriage is being forced on you, but it will work out. I sense the two of you already have feelings for each other. Right?'

Outright denial was a waste of time and breath, Gina acknowledged. Elinor was no fool.

'Of a kind,' she said.

'That's where it all starts, honey. The rest will follow. You're what Ross needs in a wife. Someone capable of standing up to him—bringing him down a peg or two.' She laughed at the expression on Gina's face. 'I'm under no illusion about my son. He's very strong-willed. To the point of arrogance at times.'

'I'd noticed,' Gina murmured.

'On the good side, he's steadfast and true to those who gain his friendship. Wives and husbands should be friends as well as lovers. Oliver was certainly mine.'

Guilt-ridden, Gina had to bite her tongue to stop herself from coming clean. Bringing Elinor down to earth with regard to this marriage would not only be cruel in the circumstances, but would also achieve nothing. Planning the wedding would give her a new lease of life these coming weeks. At least let her have that.

Roxanne failed to appear again the rest of the afternoon. Believing she had probably gone out, Gina had a shock on going up to her room to change for the evening, to find the other already there waiting for her. A very different Roxanne, smiling and apologetic.

'I've treated you badly,' she said frankly. 'I guess I was suffering from jealousy. Dad and I were always so close. I looked on him as my real father. I didn't even know about you until I got here the other day. Can you imagine the shock it was?'

'It must have been.' Gina was cautious, not at all sure where this was going. 'I felt the same when I got Grandfather's letter. I'd never had any idea what my background was.'

'Of course you didn't. It must be terrible never to have known your mother—your real mother, I mean.'

'It would have been nice to meet her,' Gina agreed, 'but there's no point fretting about it. At least I had the chance to meet my grandfather, even if it was only for a little while. And I'm sorry for the way things have worked out,' she felt bound to add. 'It never occurred to me that he'd do what he did.'

The expression that crossed the other face was come and gone too quickly for analysis. 'You must be wondering why he left me so little.'

'It isn't my business,' Gina refuted.

'He didn't like some of my friends,' Roxanne went on as if she hadn't spoken. 'He believed they were only interested in me because I'm a Harlow. This was his way of proving it.'

Gina kept her tone level. 'He thought they'd desert you once they realised you were only worth a million?'

'Exactly.' Roxanne sighed. 'Whether they do or not, I'm stuffed!'

'You owe money?' Gina hazarded.

'Afraid so. I invested in a project I thought was sound, but it fell through. The people I borrowed the money from are pressing for repayment.'

'Surely they can wait until your inheritance is through,' Gina said uncertainly.

Roxanne gave a brittle laugh. 'I only get the income, remember. I can't touch the capital.'

It was obvious now where this was going, Gina thought wryly. So much for the apparent change of heart.

'How much do you owe?' she asked.

The pause was brief. 'Three hundred.'

'That doesn't sound very bad.'

A hint of a sneer touched Roxanne's lips. 'Three hundred thousand.'

Gina gazed at her in stupefaction. The idea of borrowing that much money was crazy enough, losing it a nightmare! She hardly knew what to say.

'You're asking *me* for help?' she got out.

Roxanne spread her hands in an appealing gesture. 'I've no one else to turn to.'

'There's your mother, or Ross.'

The smile acquired a harder edge. 'I'd rather keep them out of it.'

That at least should be no surprise, Gina reflected. She lifted her shoulders in semi-apology. 'I don't see what I can do. I don't have access to any money myself until the will is proved.'

'You will have once Ross gets accounts opened for you.' Roxanne was all eagerness again, sensing victory. 'I'd be eternally grateful!'

Until the next time she found herself in financial trouble, Gina told herself. Even if she found herself in a position to come across with that amount of money, all she would be doing was giving Roxanne the idea that she was a soft touch.

'I'm sorry,' she said.

The anticipatory expression vanished, replaced by a hatred intense enough to make her take a step back. 'You'll regret this!' Roxanne spat. 'I'll make sure of it!'

If Gina had felt any sympathy at all, it was wiped out by the sheer vehemence in that statement. Roxanne didn't linger any longer, slamming the door as she left the room.

Legs shaky, Gina sank to a seat. She felt all churned up

inside. The adopted Harlows were two of a kind beneath the skin. They cared nothing for anyone but themselves.

Ross was going to learn she was no pushover too, she vowed, hardening her attitude again. She'd give him something to think about tomorrow!

The drive downtown next day was accomplished in near silence. Gina had left the screen between front and rear seats of the limousine open, but Michael seemed disinclined to converse.

She had spent a rough night, one minute tempted to throw in the towel and head for home, the next resolved to see things through to the bitter end. Money might not be the be-all and end-all, but it certainly had its uses: millions of them in this particular case.

She was nervous about the coming meeting, but determined too, deliberately lingering until there was little chance of reaching the offices in time to be in the boardroom by ten. Making an entrance, it was called.

It was already five minutes past the hour when Michael brought the car to a halt before the imposing entrance to the block. Wearing the cream suit along with high-heeled beige shoes, she felt confident enough in her appearance to swan into the reception hall as though she owned the place.

The receptionist had obviously been warned of her coming. The smile with which he directed her to a small, separate lift round a corner from the general run was dazzling. When Ross's secretary came forward to greet her when the doors opened again, Gina thought for a moment that she'd come to the wrong floor. The reception area certainly looked very similar.

'Penny, isn't it?' she said.

The other woman smiled and nodded. 'That's right. Penny Loxley. It's nice to meet you again, Miss Saxton.'

Gina returned the smile. 'My name's Virginia. Gina for short. I'd rather you called me that.'

'I'd be glad to.' Penny indicated double doors across the wide expanse of carpet. 'They're all here.'

Gina gave a laugh. 'And I'm late, on my very first morning!'

'Your privilege.' Penny wasn't attempting to hide her amusement, recognising the ploy for what it was. 'I'll take you in.'

Crossing the floor in her wake, Gina nerved herself for the coming ordeal. There were six men and two women seated at the gleaming mahogany table that stretched almost the length of the panelled room. Heads turned in unison at the opening of the door, differing expressions on every face.

The men came to their feet as Penny made what Gina considered a totally unnecessary announcement. Mentally girding her loins, she waved an airy hand.

'Please, do sit down, everyone. There's no need for formality.'

Ross viewed her expressionlessly as she made her way towards the head of the table, where he still stood. Wearing a suit similar in cut and colour to the one in which he'd greeted her at the airport, he looked the executive from head to toe. At least, she assumed so, being unable to see his feet as yet.

'You're late,' he said.

'I know.' Reaching the head of the table, she gave the occupants of it a wide smile. 'Dreadful of me to keep you all waiting. I just couldn't make up my mind what to wear!' She turned the smile full power on Ross. 'Where shall I sit?'

A dangerous glint in his eyes, he indicated the empty leather chair on his right. 'Where else would you sit?'

'Terrific!' She took the seat, looking round the assembly with overt interest. Of them all, only one face registered anything approaching benevolence. The two women, both of whom were in their fifties, wore expressions fit to turn the milk sour. Gina wondered how they'd look if she gave way to mad impulse and stuck her tongue out at the pair of them.

Ross began an introduction, going clockwise around the table. Warren Boxhall turned out to be the assumedly friendly one. Some ten years older than Ross, he was still a very attractive man. The other names all ran together in her mind. Matching them to the right faces would prove a problem for a while.

'Why don't you just carry on as though I wasn't here?' she suggested blithely when the introductions were over. 'Listen and learn is my motto! Mind you, I don't know about anyone else, but coffee would be very welcome.'

'It will be here shortly,' said Ross, sounding unruffled. 'In the meantime, we'll do as you say and carry on.'

Gina marshalled her forces over the following minutes, bent on absorbing as much as she could of the proceedings. Running an organisation the size of Harlows was certainly no sinecure.

Coffee arrived and was drunk on the hoof, as the saying went, discussion continuing apace. Gina was engrossed. This was business with a capital B! It made the boutique seem like a child's plaything.

She needed to put Barbara in the picture, came the distracting thought. She certainly wasn't going to need an income from the boutique. As the driving force behind the whole enterprise, it was only fair that her partner should benefit.

Telling her parents about the will was going to be the most difficult. The money angle they could no doubt handle, the marriage was another matter—although in their case, the impermanency would probably come as some relief.

She came back to her present surroundings to hear Ross closing the meeting. Chairs were pushed back, legs stretched, mouths exercised in low conversation as the other directors made their way from the room. It was ten to one that she was the main topic, Gina reflected.

'Just what were you playing at back there?' Ross asked on a curious note.

She gathered herself, returning his gaze with a bland expression. 'Playing at?'

'You know what I'm talking about.' He still hadn't raised his voice. 'Turning up late, acting the dumb blonde.'

'Isn't that what you take me for?' she asked.

The grey eyes took on a new expression as he studied her, his mouth slanting. 'If that's the impression I gave you the other night, I'm losing my touch. I took you to bed because it was what both of us wanted. What both of us want still, if we're honest about it. This marriage doesn't have to be a totally celibate one.'

'So far as I'm concerned, it does,' Gina retorted. 'I'm sure you'll have no difficulty in satisfying your needs outside of it. As I will myself,' she added with purpose.

There was a pause while he continued to regard her with that same enigmatic expression, then he inclined his head. 'I guess we can run with that. I'm due to take a trip to Vancouver. You'd better come too.'

'Why?' she asked, mind whirling again.

'I'd have thought it obvious. If you're going to take a responsible role in the company, you need to have some insight into the business. The Vancouver Harlow is our most recent addition. Built to order. I haven't seen it myself yet.'

'Would the company head normally do an inspection?'

'A company head does whatever he—or she—feels like doing,' he said. 'One of the perks of the job, you might say. We'll be here for the charity ball, though, so you'll still need that dress.'

Gina only heard the one word. 'You'll be going too?'

'I was going anyway.' Ross glanced at his watch. 'You'd better get moving. My mother should be here any minute, ready and eager. She never could resist a shopping spree.' His tone softened just a fraction. 'She thinks a lot of you, Gina.'

'I think a lot of her too,' she said truthfully. 'Which makes it doubly hard allowing her to think the marriage might be for real.'

'She knows it's no love match.' He made an abrupt movement. 'I'll come down with you. I've a luncheon appointment myself.'

No doubt with a woman, she thought.

Penny had been in the room throughout the meeting, taking down the minutes, her presence unobtrusive. She'd departed with the others, but was still at her desk in the outer lobby.

'Are you going to be in this afternoon,' she asked Ross, 'or shall I reschedule your three o'clock?'

'I'll be in.' He viewed her quizzically. 'There's something different about you this morning.'

'I know.' Her smile was radiant. 'I'm pregnant!'

'That's great!' Ross sounded genuinely delighted. 'You take care, now.

'She had a miscarriage last year,' he advised in the lift. 'Let's hope to God she keeps this one!'

'You're very fond of her, aren't you?' Gina remarked. She shook her head in negation as he shot her a sharp glance. 'I'm not suggesting anything beyond that.'

'Good. Penny's a lovely woman any man would fancy, but even if she weren't crazy about her husband, office affairs are strictly no go.'

'For you personally, or the company as a whole?'

'Both, for preference, although keeping tabs on all our employees would prove pretty difficult. So long as it's discreet, and doesn't interfere with work, it's easier to turn a blind eye.'

'Is this luncheon date business or pleasure?' she asked, trying to sound casual about it.

'Considering you're calling it a date rather than an appointment, I'd say you already made up your mind,' he returned drily. 'I *am* meeting a woman, as it happens. Isabel Dantry. She's one of the city's top investment bankers.'

They had reached the ground floor. Gina exited ahead of him, waving a hand to Elinor just coming through the main doors. What he'd said a few minutes ago about the marriage not necessarily being a celibate one still loomed large in her mind. Drawn to him the way she still was despite everything, was it such a bad idea? Who was to say that deeper feelings might not develop between them, given the incentive?

impression.' She dropped her hand again, self-conscious beneath his gaze. 'Are we going back to the house now?'

'I need to call in at the office first,' he said. 'It isn't far from here.'

The American notion of not far differed greatly from her own, Gina had already gathered. She was unsurprised when they took the ramp to the Hollywood Freeway after driving a couple of blocks. The traffic was heavy, with little lane discipline, though it all kept moving at a steady flow.

'Did you talk to your parents yet?' Ross asked.

'This morning,' she acknowledged. 'I told them I'd definitely be back by the weekend.'

'It's Wednesday now,' he said. 'You already booked your return flight?'

'No. But I shouldn't think there'll be much of a problem travelling first class. There were three empty seats on the way out.'

'Not to say it will be the same going east. If you're serious, you'd best get on to it. You can ring the airline from the office.'

'Can't wait to get rid of me?' she mocked.

He looked unmoved. 'You're the one determined to go.'

Which was true enough, she had to admit. It had been almost the first thing she had said to him—repeated several times since.

'I have to. I'm supposedly due back from Spain on Saturday. Barbara's going to be asking questions if I don't turn up at the shop Monday morning.'

'Why a boutique, anyway?' he asked after a moment or two. 'I'd have said you could do a whole lot better.'

'It's no little tinpot affair,' she defended. 'We cater for a pretty high-class clientele.'

'All the same—'

'All the same,' she interposed shortly, 'it's *my* choice, *my* life.'

The shrug signified a loss of interest. Gina stole a glance at the lean, hard profile, wondering what he would have said if she'd admitted to the mistake she'd made in going into the retail business at all. Barbara had carried her along with her enthusiasm, talked her into a partnership she hadn't given nearly enough thought to. Successful enough so far as it went, but not how she wanted to spend years of her life. The trouble now being that Barbara couldn't afford to buy her out, and she didn't have the wherewithal to start over in something new.

She could have, came the sneaking thought, thrust to the back of her mind where it could do least harm.

They left the freeway to cruise down a broad boulevard into the business sector of the city. Gina had anticipated something of an edifice as the headquarters of the Harlow group, but the towering glass structure bearing the insignia took her breath.

The reception lobby was sumptuously furnished, with yards of cream marble underfoot. A large curved desk occupied a central position. The uniformed receptionist on duty greeted Ross with deference as they passed on the way to the lifts.

They took the cage at the end of the row, riding all the way to the eighth floor to emerge on another, smaller, lobby area. The floor here was thickly carpeted, the decor superb in subtle tones of salmon and beige. The paintings around the walls were almost certainly originals.

The woman seated at a central desk was an oil painting herself. A year or two older than Gina, with glossy chestnut hair cut to curve about a set of beautifully balanced features, she stood up to reveal a figure to match in a plain black skirt and white blouse.

# CHAPTER FIVE

FINE feathers made fine birds indeed, Gina thought, gazing at her reflection in the cheval mirror. The pale green silk gown skimmed her body from asymmetrical neckline to ankle, outlining every curve without clinging. The sandals that went with it were mere wisps of kid leather, totteringly high yet so beautifully balanced they felt quite secure.

Her hair had been cut and styled only that morning, falling now in smooth golden abundance to her shoulders. One arm was bare, adorned only by a diamond bracelet, the other covered from shoulder to wrist. Her only other jewellery was a pair of diamond drop earrings.

For what it had all cost, she certainly should look good though! Elinor didn't know the meaning of frugality. These weren't the only things they'd purchased the other afternoon. Nor, if Elinor had anything to do with it, would they be the last. As a Harlow, she had an image to live up to.

She had seen comparatively little of Ross over the last few days. An office had been arranged for her, and a secretary allocated, but so far all she'd done was plough through reams of paperwork relating to the company. Not that she could visualise a time when she'd be capable of doing all that much else, for all her posturing.

Warren Boxhall had waited no more than a day to make the approach Elinor had anticipated. While his charm hadn't evaporated when she turned down his suggestion that they combine forces, Gina suspected that he hadn't by any means given up on the notion. If the company was floated on the market, he stood to make millions more from his shares than he could ever draw in dividends.

Ross was due any minute. They were using the limousine to take them to the charity do, along with Michael's services. It wouldn't do, Gina had gathered from Elinor, to arrive at a function like this in anything other. She was nervous, she had to admit. This was her first time out in public, so to speak. She wondered who Ross would have been taking if he weren't taking her. He would have had a wide choice for certain.

Bracing herself, she took a final glance in the mirror, then swept up the filmy stole and slim evening purse, and made for the door.

Ross had already arrived. Stomach tensing in the stark black and white, he watched her descend the stairs, eyes scanning her from top to toe with an expression she found encouraging.

'You look stunning!' he said.

'Doesn't she!' echoed Elinor with some self-congratulation, watching from a doorway.

Ross took the stole from her, hands lingering for a heartbeat as he slid it about her shoulders. Gina could feel the firm warmth of them through the fine material, stirring memories of the way they'd felt on her bare skin less than a week ago. He had to be aware of the tremor running through her.

If he was, he gave no sign of it. Elinor saw the pair of them off with satisfaction oozing from every pore. Looking rather less po-faced than usual, Michael saw them into the car before getting behind the wheel.

'Do you have to wait around to bring us back?' Gina queried when they were moving.

'Yes, ma'am,' he said.

'Not tonight,' Ross told him easily. 'We'll take a cab when we're ready.'

'That's very good of you, sir.' Michael sounded a little taken-aback. 'Lydia will be pleased.'

Ross put the screen up, indicating an end to the conversation: a move Gina found a little embarrassing.

'Don't you chat with staff?' she asked pointedly.

'Not when I have other things on my mind,' he said. 'You realise you're going to be the centre of a great deal of attention tonight? And not just for the way you look.'

'Meaning word got around about the will?' she asked after a moment.

'Meaning word got around. It's caused a stir, to say the least. You've had no media approach yet?'

'No.' Gina was alarmed. 'Am I likely to have?'

'Very much so. It's a big story. Somebody might even fancy making a film of it.'

'You're joking!'

The smile was fleeting. 'Stranger things have happened. You said you'd maybe missed your true vocation. You could play yourself.'

It was Gina's turn to smile. 'I'll pass, thanks.' She hesitated before tagging on diffidently, 'If you were planning on coming to this thing before all this happened, you must have had a partner already in mind.'

'True,' he confirmed.

'She must feel very…disgruntled about it. About it all, in fact.'

Amusement crinkled his eyes. 'That's one way of putting it.'

'But you'll have told her the marriage is only temporary, of course.'

'I see no reason to tell anyone,' he said. 'It's strictly between the two of us.'

'You really don't give a damn, do you?' Gina accused.

Leaning comfortably into the corner of his seat, Ross regarded her with ironically lifted brows. 'Why the surprise? You had me down for a bastard less than twenty-four hours after we met.'

'Sound judgement,' she returned caustically. 'Women are obviously just cannon fodder to you!'

His mouth curved again. 'You certainly have a way with words! I wouldn't say I'd sown any more wild oats than other men my age.'

'But marriage never figured on the agenda.'

'In this town, it's a path to disaster.'

'Your mother and Oliver lasted pretty well,' she pointed out.

'The exception, not the rule.' There was a pause, a subtle change of tone. 'How did your folks take the news?'

More a desire for a change of subject than any real interest, Gina conjectured. 'I didn't tell them yet,' she admitted reluctantly.

Dark brows drew together. 'Why not?'

'I'm still having difficulty accepting it all myself.' That was certainly no lie. 'I'm planning to ring them tomorrow.'

'Your partner too—assuming you haven't told her either?'

'Barbara too.'

'You still intend handing over the business to her wholesale?'

'Of course,' she said. 'I'm hardly going to need the income.'

'True enough. All the same, it's a gesture many wouldn't be prepared to make. I hope she appreciates it.'

Right now, Gina had other concerns on her mind. Another few minutes, and she would be facing a world she'd hitherto only seen on screen: the centre of attention, Ross had warned. It was going to take every ounce of self-confidence she could muster to get her through the coming hours—to say nothing of the days and weeks following. Why, oh, why had she agreed to this fiasco?

The event was being held at the downtown Harlow. Flashbulbs started popping the moment they alighted from the car, while a host of clamouring journalists pressed in around them. Ross handled it all with aplomb, whisking her straight through to the hotel foyer.

Gina hadn't been in the place before this, and was impressed with its size and dignified splendour. Ross was greeted from all sides as they mingled with the crowd already occupying the spacious lobby, fielding the comments with an insouciance Gina wished she could emulate. She lost count of names and faces, although she recognised several stars of film and television. She felt totally overwhelmed. Never in a million years could she fit in to this environment, she thought depressedly.

But then, she wasn't going to need to, was she? Not for long, at any rate.

Two television crews were filming the arrivals. Ross avoided one presenter making a beeline for them by steering her into a lift about to close its doors. He left his hand where it was under her elbow as they rose to the top floor. The heels she was wearing brought her eyes on a level with his jawline. She could see the smooth, firm line on the periphery of her vision, catch the faint scent of his aftershave. The tension inside her at the moment had nothing to do with nerves.

Lit by glittering chandeliers, the huge room scintillated with crystal and silver, the carpet underfoot so thick, Gina could feel her heels sinking half an inch into it. Their table was way up at the front on the edge of the dance floor, with yet another gauntlet to run by way of the people already seated there. The smile on her face felt permanently etched.

Two of the other couples were mere acquaintances, she gathered. Both in their thirties, Meryl and Jack Thornton were old friends, involved in real estate. They put her at ease immediately, whatever curiosity they might feel kept under bounds.

Gina found the sumptuous five-course meal more than a little incongruous considering the purpose for which the event was being held. There was dancing between courses. Held close in Ross's arms, the hard muscularity of his thighs against hers, she felt the tension mounting. She could tell herself he was an out-and-out swine until the cows came home, but it made absolutely no difference to the effect he was having on her. She wanted him desperately.

The brush of his lips against her cheek almost finished her. 'Keep feeling the same way,' he murmured against her skin. 'The evening won't last for ever.'

She should tell him to get lost, she knew, but she couldn't summon the necessary strength of mind. That he could still find her desirable in a room containing so much feminine beauty was a stimulus in itself. Why not make the most of what time they had together? she asked herself. Cliché it might be, but half a loaf was still better than none.

It was coming up to midnight before the main purpose of the evening was brought to the fore. The charity was for children in need. Gina wasn't all that surprised to hear Harlows announced as one of the main sponsors. The devastation came when she was asked up along with Ross to front the appeal for further donations from those present.

'Bear with it,' he murmured as they made their way forward.

She did, though only just. Keeping a smile on her face, knowing speculation was rife throughout the whole assembly, was one of the most arduous things she'd ever done. She envied the ease with which Ross launched into a brief spiel about the aims of the charity, only too thankful that she wasn't called on to say anything herself.

Both cheques and cash were deposited in the baskets that were circulated among the guests with a readiness she found admirable. The people here were all of them moneyed, but that didn't necessarily foster philanthropy.

'I keep trying to persuade Ross to invest in a property,' Meryl declared when the two of them visited the powder room together a little later, 'but he won't play. Not that I can blame him too much, considering his place. Terrific, isn't it?'

'I haven't seen it yet,' Gina admitted.

'You haven't?' Meryl sounded surprised. 'I'd have thought...' She broke off, shaking her head in self-recrimination. 'Forget it.'

Gina took the bull by the horns. 'You don't have to keep treading lightly round the subject. It has to be a pretty general topic at the moment.'

Meryl laughed, obviously relieved. 'You could say that! It's been a bit of a shock, I have to admit. Even more so for Ross, I imagine. He's managed to steer well clear of marriage up to now. Not for want of trying by at least one person I could mention.'

Gina concentrated on applying lipstick. 'No one here tonight?'

'I guess she would have been if you hadn't come into the picture. She'll be fuming. No man puts Dione Richards aside—even for a future wife!'

Gina felt her stomach turn over. '*The* Dione Richards?' she asked.

'The one and only. You've seen her films?'

'A couple of them.'

'Hardly the world's greatest actress, but good box office. One look into those big baby blues and men turn to mush! Jack no exception,' she added drily. She viewed Gina appraisingly through the mirror. 'You aren't at the back of the line when it comes to looks yourself. Terrific figure too! Lucky Ross. He could have been stuck with a real plain Jane.'

For what difference it made, Gina reflected on the way back to the table. Dione Richards had been voted the most beautiful woman in the world only last year. Who could compete with that?

The intimate little smile Ross gave her on her return to the table was a boost nevertheless. Dione might have the edge on looks, but she didn't have the man. Not tonight, at any rate. She was probably being all kinds of a fool in contemplating what she was contemplating, but she couldn't help herself. She wanted him. Right now, that was all she could think about.

People were already beginning to leave. Gina was more than half expecting the suggestion that they call it a day themselves. From the look in Meryl's eyes when they took their leave, the other woman was well aware of where they were heading. She schooled herself not to care. She was doing what a whole lot of others did for once, and seizing the moment.

There was a cab already waiting. Gina made no demur when Ross told the driver to take them to the Beverly Hills Harlow. She held nothing back when he drew her to him to kiss her.

'I've been wanting to do that all evening,' he said against her hair.

'So why didn't you?' she murmured. 'Plenty of others were kissing.'

His laugh was low-pitched. 'I don't believe in starting something I can't finish.'

The champagne she had consumed was making her head swim; the movement of the car wasn't helping. She made an effort to focus her mind on other things.

'Neither do I,' she said.

He kissed her again, teasing her lips apart with the tip of his tongue and bringing the blood hammering into her ears. The silky probing of the soft inner flesh was electrifying. She felt a dampness between her thighs, a spasming in her groin: sensations that for the present overrode everything else.

It was only when she got out of the car at the hotel that the nausea began to make itself felt. She did her best to tamp the queasiness down. It would pass, she assured herself. She hadn't had all that much.

There were few people in the lobby. Even so, Gina was aware of eyes following the pair of them as they made their way to a small, obviously private lift off the main concourse. The motion as they rose was of no assistance whatsoever. She could only hope and pray that she wouldn't throw up.

She had only the vaguest impression of her surroundings when Ross opened the door. He'd made no attempt at conversation in the lift, nor did he say anything now. He took her arm and steered her to another door leading off the entrance hall, opening it to reveal a bathroom. Right then, Gina had but the one thought in mind. She made it just in time.

It seemed an age before the retching stopped. Even then, her head wouldn't stop whirling. How could she have been so stupid? she thought miserably. She'd told Ross she didn't like champagne, when what she should have said was that it generally didn't like her. Ignoring that danger simply because everyone else was drinking the stuff and she needed the boost was ridiculous.

Well, she was paying for it now. She must be the first woman he had ever brought back here who'd finished up with her head stuck down a toilet bowl! The mere thought of facing him after this was enough to stir nausea again.

It had to be done, of course. She could hardly stay in here all night. A face and mouth rinse went some small way towards refreshing her, but there was no denying the unsteadiness still in her limbs when she finally emerged from the bathroom.

Waiting in the hallway, Ross viewed her with apparently solicitous enquiry. 'Better?' he asked.

Gina nodded, not trusting her voice, wishing she hadn't as pain spliced through her head.

'Obviously not,' he said, seeing her wince. 'Feeling dizzy?'

There was no point denying it when every step she took betrayed the fact. 'I'm sorry about this,' she got out.

His shrug was dismissive. 'It happens. I should have remembered what you said about not liking champagne.'

'I didn't have to drink it,' she responded. 'If you'll call a cab, I—'

'You can't go anywhere like that,' he cut in decisively. 'You'd better use the spare room for tonight, and we'll see how you feel in the morning.'

'I can't...' she began, desisting abruptly as her stomach contracted again. There was no way she dared get in a car feeling this way. 'I'm sorry,' she repeated. 'I know you were expecting...'

There was irony in the smile that touched his lips as she let the words trail away. 'I'll get over it. Think you can make it to the bedroom—or shall I carry you?'

'I'm a bit dizzy, not paralytic!' she said, seeking refuge

in humour, however weak. 'What about your mother? Won't she be concerned if I don't turn up?'

'I doubt it.' The irony was there in his voice this time.

Meaning Elinor would probably have taken it for granted that the two of them would be spending the night together, Gina assumed. And why not? They were both adults. The fact that right now she felt anything but was another story.

The bedroom he took her to was large and beautifully furnished, the two beds queen sized. There was an *en suite*, Ross pointed out.

'Can you cope OK?' he asked from the doorway.

Gina forced herself to look at him directly. He had taken off both jacket and tie while she'd been in the bathroom, and loosened the collar of his pristine white dress shirt. Hair ruffled as though from the passage of a hand through it, he looked like a man who'd undergone, and was probably still undergoing, severe frustration. Hardly to be wondered at considering the way she'd been in the car.

'I'll be fine,' she said, wishing she could believe it. 'Goodnight, Ross. And…thanks.'

'No problem.'

He closed the door softly between them, leaving her standing there biting her lip. She'd made a total fool of herself, and for what? Ross wasn't going to develop any deeper feelings than he'd already shown for her. There was every possibility that after tonight, he wouldn't want to know anyway.

She awoke to the faint sound of music. Memory brought a swift return of last night's depression, forcibly overcome. There was nothing to be gained from wallowing in it.

Lifting her head cautiously from the pillows, she was relieved to feel no more than a faint tightness behind her eyes. She might deserve to suffer a hangover, but it would have been more than she could cope with.

Surprisingly, it was only a little gone eight o'clock. The dress she'd taken off last night was slung over a chair: the thought of putting it on again was anathema to her, but she didn't have much choice.

She'd slept nude. Taking up the scanty lace bra and matching panties, she went through to the *en suite*, regarding her bleary-eyed appearance in wry distaste. Her hair didn't look too bad, and would look even better with a brush through, but all she had in her purse was a lipstick. Not that Ross was likely to give a damn how she looked this morning.

She took a shower, and donned her underwear. The long white towelling bathrobe hung on the door was just about her size. Obviously kept ready for female visitors using the spare bathroom, Gina thought, and took it. It went against the grain to wear something others had worn before her— even if it did smell freshly laundered—but at least it saved her from putting on the dress again right away.

The music was still playing when she left the bedroom. Double doors gave access to a living area the size of a football field, with floor-to-ceiling windows providing a superb view out to the mountains.

Wearing a silk robe over what appeared to be black pyjama trousers, Ross was seated at a table on the balcony that ran the whole width of the room. He looked up from his newspaper as she emerged, the lift of his eyebrow asking the question.

'I'm OK,' she said, reluctant to look at him directly. 'Is that coffee I can smell?'

He took up the pot without answering, and poured another cup, pushing it across to her as she took a seat.

'You look like a well-scrubbed schoolgirl,' he observed.

'I feel like a thoroughly chastised one,' she returned. 'I should have had more sense!'

'If wishes were horses,' he quoted. 'I've over-indulged too many times in the past myself to come the heavy.'

'But not to the same extent, I'll bet.'

'I was lucky enough to finish up with just a bad head. You don't have to flay yourself. You're not the first, you won't be the last.'

She glanced at him from beneath her lashes, every sense alive to the impact of the lean-featured, freshly shaved face. The robe revealed a glimpse of sun-kissed bare chest. She touched the tip of her tongue to dry lips.

'Hungry?' he asked, jerking her head up. She met his eyes in some confusion, sure he must know exactly what was going through her mind.

If he did, he was keeping it to himself. His expression was devoid of irony.

'A bit,' she admitted. 'Do you have a kitchen?'

'There's a service area behind the screen over there,' indicating the far side of the room. 'I make my own coffee and toast, or even occasionally produce a full breakfast, but I use Room Service for everything else when I'm in. What do you fancy?'

'Toast sounds good. I can make it myself,' she added quickly.

The smile was brief. 'I've no intention of stopping you. You can do me a couple of slices while you're at it.'

She went back inside to cross to the screened area, finding time on the way to appraise the light, modern decor. The furnishings were Scandinavian, she guessed, the quality outstanding. But then, what else would she expect?

As anticipated, the kitchen—or service area, as Ross preferred to call it—was well-equipped with both storage and appliances, including a typical American refrigerator-freezer big enough to house a whole family's food for a year. Gina took a peep inside while she was waiting for the toast to cook, finding it somewhat sparsely stocked. No point in keeping a lot of food around, she supposed, if Ross didn't do much cooking for himself.

There had been no butter on the table out there, from what she could recall. She put a dish of the small individual packs on a tray along with a selection of preserves and the rack of toast, added cutlery and bore the whole lot outside.

'Very domesticated,' Ross commented, eyeing the spread.

Gina found a laugh, determined to carry this through with nonchalance—no matter how spurious. 'The product of my upbringing.'

He took a piece of the toast and spread butter on it, ignoring the preserves. 'Maybe something to be said for it after all.'

'I hardly see you settling for a domesticated lifestyle,' she said lightly.

'There could be advantages.'

'Like having a woman available at all times?'

The tilt of a lip brought sudden warmth to her cheeks. She hadn't meant to say that, it had just slipped out.

'Not that you've ever had any difficulty in that direction, of course,' she added, digging herself an even deeper hole.

'I did last night,' he observed. He watched her colour rise with a certain relish. 'You still owe me.'

'I owe you nothing!' she retorted, resenting the implication. 'I'm sorry if you were frustrated, but like you said a while ago, it happens!'

The grey eyes mocked her anger. 'Calm down. I'm not claiming immediate reparation. In fact, I'll be taking you back to Buena Vista shortly. We're leaving for Vancouver this afternoon.'

Gina gazed at him in stunned silence for a moment, the wind taken completely from her sails. She'd forgotten completely about the proposed trip. Even if she'd remembered, she wouldn't have expected it to be quite this soon.

'We'll be taking one of the company jets, so there's no hard and fast timetable,' Ross continued. 'You'll need enough for two or three days. You might want to stick a swimsuit in too. The Vancouver Harlow has three pools.'

Gina found her voice with an effort. 'I really can't see the point in my coming with you.'

'Experience,' he said. 'If you're serious about staying on board after the divorce, you need all you can get.'

'If that's meant to remind me that the marriage will only be temporary, it isn't necessary!' she flashed. 'I wouldn't try denying the physical attraction, but that's as far as it goes for me too.'

'Then we've neither of us anything to worry about,' he returned, unmoved. 'Better eat your toast, before it goes completely cold.'

Gina forbore from further comment. Refusing out of hand to accompany him on this trip would call for reasons she wasn't prepared to give. For all his talk of owing him, she doubted if he meant it. Seeing her drunk and incapable last night, and scrubbed clean like a schoolgirl this morning—as he'd so delicately put it—was enough to put any man off for life.

She finished the toast with little appetite. There was a canopy over the part of the balcony they were occupying, affording shade from the full glare of the sun, but the heat was steadily rising. Green and verdant, the mountains looked cool and inviting.

'You can go up there another day,' Ross said, following

the direction of her gaze. He pushed back his chair and got to his feet, not bothering to catch the belt of his robe as the two ends slid silkily apart. 'I'll go and get dressed. See you in ten.'

Gina stayed right where she was. It was hardly going to take her any time at all to throw on the only garment available to her. The glimpse she'd just had of that well-toned body had set every nerve-end tingling again. She needed a moment or two to bring her pulse rate down.

The way she felt at present, a flight home was a more sensible course than the trip to Vancouver. Except that sense didn't come into it. She'd committed herself by accepting the condition in the first place. The future of the company was at stake too. Warren couldn't be allowed to gain control.

She had to force herself to move in the end. The door to what she assumed was Ross's bedroom was partly ajar when she went out into the hall. From the sound of it, he was on the phone, his tone lightly placatory.

'Naturally I would. It was unavoidable in the circumstances. I'm going to be out of town for a few days, but I'll give you a call as soon as I get back.'

Gina continued on her way feeling even more disconsolate. That was Dione Richards he was talking to, for certain. She filled in the unspoken part of the first overheard sentence, 'Naturally I would rather have been with you.' He almost certainly wouldn't have suffered the frustration she had inflicted on him.

He was ready and waiting in jeans and a T-shirt when she emerged wearing the green dress.

'Is there a back way out?' she asked. 'If I have to cross the lobby in this, everyone will know I spent the night here.'

'The staff will know anyway. Hotel grapevines are second to none.' Ross sounded unconcerned. 'There is a back way, but I can't guarantee a clear run. Hold your head up and look them straight in the eye. It's nobody's business but ours.'

All very well for him to talk, she thought sourly.

They descended to the ground floor without speaking, emerging round the corner from the main concourse and heading down a long corridor lined with doors. Expecting one of them to open any minute, Gina drew a breath of relief when they turned another corner to traverse a narrower corridor, with windows overlooking the rear of the hotel. Ross pushed a pair of fire doors open to afford an exit onto a large paved area backed by a line of huge bins.

'Stay here, if you're still feeling sensitive, and I'll fetch the cab I ordered round for you,' he said.

'Cab?' she queried.

The glance he gave her was impatient. 'I left my car up at the house. If I take another, that's going to be stuck there too.'

'Of course.' She summoned a smile. 'You're right, I'm being ridiculous. I'll come with you.'

It took a few minutes to walk round to the front of the place. Her bravado went into swift decline when she saw all the comings and goings, revived by sheer force of will. Head up, she stalked to the waiting cab, ignoring the glances cast her way.

Like cabbies the world over, the driver showed no reaction to her appearance, but simply put the vehicle into motion. If she'd been on her own, Gina could have relaxed a little; with Ross seated beside her, there was no chance. The effect he had on her was unchanged by last night's fiasco. The merest brush of his bare arm against hers sent a surge like an electric shock through her body. She wished she'd never slept with him at all. What wasn't known couldn't be missed.

# CHAPTER SIX

IT WAS almost ten when they reached the house. Ross declined to come indoors with her.

'I've things to see to before we go,' he said. 'I'll pick you up at two. Wear something—'

'Comfortable,' Gina finished for him. 'Yes, I know.'

She didn't wait to see him drive off. There was no one around when she went inside. She made her bedroom in double-quick time, closing the door in some small relief.

The dress left ready to be taken for cleaning, she slid into a pair of jeans and pulled a T-shirt over her head, before turning her attention to the question of packing. Two or three days, Ross had said. A pretty lengthy tour of inspection.

The only suitcase she had available was the one she'd brought with her just two weeks ago. She chose clothes at random from the selection now in the wardrobes, picking out a lightweight trouser suit to wear on the plane. This was a business trip, nothing else. From now on, she concentrated all her attention in that direction.

It was still only eleven. Leaving her face bare of make-up for the present, she made her way back downstairs to seek Elinor.

The latter was under an umbrella down on the pool deck. She looked up from her book with a welcoming smile.

'Hi! How long have you been back?'

'About an hour.' Gina sank to a seat on a nearby lounger, eyeing the older woman with some reserve. 'Aren't you going to ask what happened?'

Elinor laughed. 'Honey, the way you looked last night, I don't need to ask! I knew the two of you were made for each other the first time I saw you together. Maybe it isn't exactly the ideal way to start a marriage, but you'll make a go of it. You're off to a good start already.'

Torn by guilt again, Gina opted for some light relief. 'I wouldn't be too sure about that. I drank too much champagne and made myself ill. I spent the night in Ross's guest room.'

'Poor Ross!' Elinor's eyes were sparkling. 'He must be feeling really deprived! Not that you need worry. Starvation only increases the appetite. Are you packed yet?'

Gina looked at her blankly. 'You knew about this afternoon?'

'Only since last night. Ross told me while we were waiting for you to come down. He's planning to spend the weekend on Vancouver Island after you get through vetting the new place apparently. It will be good for the two of you to have a couple of days on your own together.

'I'm going to start needing your help with the wedding plans when you get back,' she added. 'The organisers have everything in hand with regard to the church and reception, but we have to get your dress chosen. There isn't going to be time to have it made, but we'll find something suitable. What about bridesmaids?'

Gina shook her head, hardly knowing what to say.

'I've a cousin with twin daughters your age, if you've no one else in mind. They'd be thrilled to do it!'

'That would be great.'

The wedding was the last thing Gina wanted to talk about—the last thing she wanted to think about right now. If Ross hadn't already aborted the Vancouver Island idea, he could forget it. A celibate relationship offered far fewer pitfalls.

Clad casually himself in trousers and open-necked shirt, with a light linen jacket, he arrived at five minutes to the hour.

'Glad to see you took me at my word,' he commented, approving the suit. He glanced down at the smallish suitcase she'd handed him. 'Is this it?'

'You said two or three days,' she returned.

'And you believe in travelling light. I should have remembered.' He looked at his mother. 'I'll call tonight. Are you going to be OK?'

A bit late to be thinking of that, Gina thought, although Elinor didn't seem concerned.

'I'll be fine,' she assured him. 'I'm out to dinner tonight, meeting a group for lunch tomorrow, and attending a charity affair in the afternoon, so I'll be pretty busy. I'll look forward to hearing all about it when you get back,' she added to Gina.

On impulse, Gina went over and kissed her on the cheek. 'I'll keep a daily diary,' she promised.

Ross glanced at his watch. 'I know I said time wasn't pressing, but I'd like to at least get in the air before dark!'

'Patience,' admonished his mother, 'is a virtue!'

'The beggar's virtue.' He opened the front passenger door of the waiting car. 'Ready?'

Gina slid into the seat feeling anything but, pulses dancing the usual fandango as the scent of his aftershave tantalised her nostrils. No backsliding, she told herself resolutely. She couldn't afford to become any more involved than she already was.

Seating eight, the sleek private jet was all soft leather and walnut inside. Apart from a slight detour to avoid a storm front building over the Sierra Nevada range, they made good time, landing at Vancouver at six-thirty.

There was a limousine waiting to take them directly to the hotel. Impressive enough from the outside, the latter was even more so inside, the lobby alone a symphony in glass and sumptuous carpeting. Unlike the general chains, every Harlow was designed differently to suit its intended clientele: an individuality that had helped make the company name what it was. Gina very much approved of those differences herself. She'd stayed in hotels where even the pictures on the bedroom walls were obviously out of a job lot spread around the chain.

They were greeted with deference by the general manager himself, and efficiently roomed in adjoining suites. There were connecting doors between the two, Gina noted, securely locked at present.

Ross had elected to have dinner in one of the four restaurants. Dressing for it in a simple linen tunic that had cost enough to have kept her for a month back home, she went back over the flight in her mind's eye.

Conversation had proved surprisingly easy. Ross had even refrained from ironic comment when she'd asked the hostess looking after them for an orange juice instead of champagne. It seemed pretty obvious that he'd lost interest in persuing the physical side of their relationship, for which she could hardly blame him. What she needed to do was foster the same attitude.

One look at him when he called for her, tall, dark and devastating in a silver-grey suit, and she was forced to acknowledge herself a lost cause. She would just have to live with it, she thought resignedly.

'Nice outfit,' he commented.

'I try,' she said, wondering how she could sound so collected when every part of her yearned for contact with that hard, masculine body. 'I imagine word will have gone round by now that you're in the building.'

'That *we're* in the building,' he corrected. 'Having the general manager check us in will have set the ball in motion. I'd have preferred him to keep it low-key.'

'So that you could see how the place was being run without people knowing who you are?' she hazarded, eliciting a brief smile.

'The departmental heads are hand-picked. Poached from other hotels in some cases. For what they're being paid, I think they can be trusted to keep things running smoothly, whether we're here or not. I haven't noted a single thing to complain about as yet. The way it should be.' His voice briskened. 'If you're ready.'

The chosen restaurant was on the first floor—second here, Gina reminded herself—and already well populated. While he addressed them both by name, the *maître d'* refrained from making any deferential show as he saw them seated. Their table was in an alcove affording privacy from their immediate neighbours. A prior arrangement on Ross's part, Gina fancied.

Pristine white damask cloths set with sparkling crystal and silverware made an excellent impression. An arrangement of seasonal flowers occupied central position: renewed every day, judging from their unblemished appearance. The lighting was designed to cast a soft glow over every table: enough to see what was being eaten, but immensely flattering to the skin.

'It's all so beautifully done,' Gina commented. She gave a laugh, determined to keep her end up. 'If you'd told me even a month ago that I'd be living it up on this level, I'd never have believed it!'

Ross regarded her with tolerant expression. 'You'll get accustomed to it. A few more months, and you'll be taking it all for granted.'

'The way you do?' she said, shying away from thoughts of that future.

'It's been a part of my life for the last twenty years. The first fourteen weren't exactly on the breadline either. My father was a banker. A bit of a womaniser too, unfortunately. And if you say, like father, like son, I'll put you across my knee,' he threatened.

'What, here?' she asked. 'That would be a new kind of floor show!'

He laughed. 'Are you ever stuck fast for an answer?'

'Only when I'm drunk.' She pulled a wry face. 'I felt a total wreck this morning!'

'You looked remarkably far from it,' he said. 'Few women can get away with a bare face in bright sunlight—especially after spending half the night throwing up.'

'It wasn't half the night,' she said in mock indignation, trying not to read too much into the compliment. 'It just felt like it.'

'Forget it,' he advised. 'I'm going to.'

The arrival of the wine waiter took his attention. Not about to take any risks, Gina asked for a kir. Ross ordered a bottle of some wine she didn't recognise by name for himself.

She watched him as he spoke to the waiter, unable to conquer the inner turmoil. His mouth was so sensual; she could feel it on hers, nibbling, teasing; tongue flickering delicately between her lips, enticing her to respond in kind. She'd always hated French kissing, but with Ross it was so different, so utterly alluring. She ached to be with him again, nude in his arms, his hands exploring her body.

She came down to earth to find him watching her curiously, the waiter departed. 'I asked you if you'd decided what you'd like to eat yet,' he said.

Gina was grateful once more for the subdued lighting.

'Sorry, I was miles away. I'll have the melon and the salmon,' she added, plumping for the first dishes that sprang to mind.

She kept a firmer grip on herself during the meal, turning the conversation to the company. Ross answered all her questions readily enough.

'Did you call your parents?' he asked over coffee.

'I didn't have time,' she said.

'You had at least a couple of hours after I dropped you at the house,' he pointed out. 'Don't you think it time you put them in the picture?'

Gina made a helpless little gesture. 'It's going to be such a shock for them.'

'It's going to be that whatever time you call.' He paused, adding when she failed to reply, 'Do you want me to do it for you?'

'That would be even worse! I'll do it tomorrow.'

'What are you going to tell them?'

'No more than I have to. Like your mother, they'd be devastated to know what the plan really is. You do realise she's taking it for granted the...arrangement will be permanent?'

'I'd rather gained that impression, yes.'

'Are you willing to tell her the truth?'

'No,' he admitted. 'Not yet, at any rate. It's helping her through a bad time. Best you let your parents assume the same for now.'

He was so matter-of-fact about it all, Gina thought hollowly.

'We should have had the quick civil ceremony you wanted,' she said. 'The whole thing is getting out of hand.'

'Too late now,' Ross observed. 'You'll just have to put up with it. Me too, unfortunately.'

'Are there likely to be a lot of guests?' she asked after a moment.

'With my mother compiling the list, at least a couple of hundred.'

'Some from the film world too?'

'From all sources. Excluding Karin Trent, if that's who you've got in mind,' he added drily.

It wasn't Karin she was thinking of, but she let it pass. If it was true that Dione Richards had designs on Ross herself, it was unlikely that she'd be attending either. Not that the wedding would necessarily put a stop to their association. For all she knew, Ross had already told the woman he'd soon be free again.

It was only a little after ten, but she had had enough. 'I think I'm going to turn in,' she said. 'I didn't get all that much sleep last night.'

'Sure.' Ross came to his feet along with her. 'An early night will do us both good.'

Her heart rate increased, dropping again as she met the dispassionate grey eyes. Whatever attraction she'd had for him, it was so obviously dead and gone.

There were plenty of people still milling around the lobby. They took an interior lift rather than the glass one that climbed the outside of the building, losing people at each floor to arrive at their own as sole occupants.

The suite Gina was occupying was first in line. She fished the keycard from her purse with unsteady hands, dropping it on the carpet. Ross picked it up and inserted it in the slot, pushing open one of the double doors to allow her access.

'See you at breakfast,' he said, and moved on. leaving her standing there feeling thoroughly depressed. It made better sense to keep things on a purely businesslike level, she knew, but the way Ross made her feel, the coming weeks were going to be hell to live through.

Breakfast was delivered to the suite with speed and efficiency. Gina took it on trust that the regular guests would receive the same service. A hotel of this calibre couldn't afford any less.

Ross would be planning a tour of the place today, she assumed. She'd accompany him because it would be expected of her, and do her best to act the part she'd been allocated. She was, after all, a major stock-holder. Or would be, once the marriage licence was signed.

She was finishing her coffee when Ross arrived at nine. He was wearing the same suit he'd worn last night, though with a different shirt and tie, and looked ready for business.

'The GM is taking us on a tour of the place,' he said. 'I'd as soon do it without him, but the suggestion might not go down very well.'

'You're the big boss,' Gina returned with deliberated flippancy. 'Your word is surely his command!'

'Not if we want to keep him.' The emphasis on the 'we' was slight. 'Conroy was persuaded to put off retirement for a couple of years to take the job on. I'm told he can be touchy.'

He took in the table bearing the remnants of her breakfast. 'I see you had Room Service too. How did you find it?'

'Excellent. Not that I'd have expected anything less.' She briskened her voice to add, 'You don't really need me on the tour. I'd probably just get in the way. I thought I might take a look at the shopping arcade down on mezzanine. From the glimpse I got of it last night, it's certainly worth visiting.'

'You can shop any time,' he said decisively. 'Conroy would take it as a personal insult.'

Mr Conroy could go run up a shutter! she thought, but refrained from voicing the sentiment. 'That definitely wouldn't do,' she said instead, keeping the sarcasm low-key. 'Still, I don't suppose it's going to take all day?'

'I'd doubt it.' Ross studied her, a glimmer of what could have been derision deep down in the grey eyes. 'I have to go out myself later this afternoon. You'll have plenty of time to look round the arcade then.'

'Business?' she asked before she could stop herself, and saw the glimmer become a definite gleam.

'Of a kind. I'll be back in good time for dinner.'

Which you'll be eating alone, she felt like telling him. That he would be seeing some woman, she didn't doubt. Like a sailor, he probably had one stashed in every port!

The tour took her mind off her personal problems for a while. For the first time, she began to realise just how much went into the running of a large hotel. Ross found no major fault in any department, much to James Conroy's gratification.

They had lunch in his private quarters, along with the assistant general manager. Tall and fair-haired, Neil Baxter was in his mid-thirties. Young for his position, Gina gathered, though obviously more than capable. She found him perhaps a bit too much on the serious side, but pleasant enough.

Ross left the hotel at three, still without saying where he was going. Not that she had any right to know, Gina conceded hollowly. They were both of them free agents.

Try as she might to stop it, her imagination went into overdrive over the next hour. If it was a woman he was seeing, they would almost certainly be in bed by now. She could visualise the scene: the clothing scattered across the floor; the writhing naked bodies. She'd no right to the jealousy sweeping her, but it was all-consuming.

Holding several top-class shops, the arcade provided some slight distraction. The prices in the boutique still appeared pretty exorbitant to her, though it seemed churlish not to buy anything, with the assistants so eager to see her suited. She settled for a skirt and long-sleeved top in her favourite cream, leaving them to be delivered to her suite.

Neil Baxter was passing as she emerged from the shop. 'We serve English tea in the Empress lounge,' he said, on realising she was on her own. 'I often take advantage myself. Perhaps you'd join me?'

Glad of any company at present, Gina was only too ready to take him up on the invitation.

The lounge was already well occupied. Tea was served to individual tables on silver trays in finest china, with a tempting selection of sandwiches and cakes. Judging from the snippets of conversation filtering across, it wasn't just English clientele who availed themselves of the service.

'We get all nationalities,' Neil confirmed. 'Even those who'd never normally drink the stuff. It's the ambience they like. There's something very civilised about afternoon tea.'

He accepted the cup Gina had poured for him, making an appreciative face as he took a sip. 'Excellent!'

'Just like back home,' Gina concurred.

There was a pause. When Neil spoke again it was a little tentatively. 'Is it true that you and Mr Harlow are just business partners?'

She should tell him it was none of *his* business, Gina knew, but she was sick of the pretence. 'True enough,' she said. 'A marriage of convenience, it's called.'

She regretted it the moment the words left her lips, but it was too late for retraction. Not that it mattered a deal, she defended. The only one with any illusions about the marriage was too far away for the grapevine to reach. Anyway, even Elinor would have to know some time.

'So I can ask you out to dinner without crossing any demarcation lines,' Neil confirmed.

Caught on the hop, Gina sought refuge in humour. 'You Canadians certainly don't waste any time!'

'Nothing ventured, nothing gained,' he returned.

In no way blind to the fact that her position was probably the main draw, her first inclination was to refuse. On the other hand, she thought, why not take advantage of the opportunity to show Ross *she* wasn't stuck fast for companionship either? Why should she be expected to hang around until he deigned to put in an appearance?

'Nice idea,' she said before she could change her mind. 'But not here.'

'Of course.' Neil sounded agreeable to anything. 'I know just the place. What time would you like to eat?'

'Let's make it early,' she suggested. 'Seven?'

'Fine by me. I'll have a cab waiting at ten before. It's only a short drive away.'

She was doing this for all the wrong reasons, Gina thought ruefully, but she couldn't back out now. Anyway, it was doubtful if Neil had anything but his own business interests in mind.

There was no sound from the adjoining suite when she finally went up at six—even with her ear pressed against the communicating door. She thought of pushing a note under the door, abandoning the idea on the grounds that she owed Ross no explanation. For all she knew, he'd be out all night.

Being so much further north, it was a great deal cooler here than in LA. She donned the skirt and top already delivered, topping them with a short beige jacket she'd brought with her and sliding her feet into high-heeled leather sandals. She'd already acquired a touch of Los Angeles gloss, she acknowledged, studying her smooth, shining hair and flawless make-up in the mirror. All down to Elinor's efforts.

Neil was waiting for her in the lobby at a quarter to the hour. He viewed her with open appreciation as she crossed the wide expanse to join him, seemingly oblivious to the glances drawn their way from the duty staff. Gina had the distinct feeling that she was something of a trophy.

As he'd said, the restaurant he'd chosen was only a short distance away. It was small, intimate and very up-market, and its menus bore no prices. She agreed without much interest when he suggested they share the Châteaubriand, not really in the mood for eating at all.

Stilted at first, conversation eased a little over the course of the meal. Gina avoided any personal probing into her own background by encouraging him to talk about himself, which he wasn't all that loath to do.

'A couple of years, and I'll be ready to take over from James when he finally retires,' he said, after filling her in on his progress since leaving university. 'Not that I invited you out in the hope of advancing my career,' he added hastily.

'It hadn't occurred to me,' Gina assured him, lying through her teeth. 'I'm sure you'll make a fine GM.'

They were on to the coffee stage when the call came through. Neil pulled a wry face as he slipped the mobile back into his pocket. 'Afraid I'm needed. Some kind of problem with one of the convention groups.'

'Duty comes first,' she said, grateful for a reason to end the evening.

It was still only a little after nine when they reached the hotel. Neil went immediately to deal with whatever had blown up, leaving Gina to make her way to her suite. It

Ross had returned, he would probably be at dinner in one
or other of the restaurants. If he hadn't yet come back, it
was likely that he'd be spending the night out.

Not that she could care less what he did from now on,
she told herself unconvincingly.

The maid who had turned down her bed last night had
left lamps lit throughout the suite. Gina came to an abrupt
stop on seeing Ross lounging in a chair.

'The wanderer returns!' he observed.

Gina recovered her voice, and something of her wits.
'How did you get in here?'

'I had the communicating doors opened up.' He viewed
her from head to foot and back again, gaze coming to rest
on her face with an expression she found disquieting. 'I
said I'd be back for dinner.'

'Did you? I must have forgotten.' She kept her tone in-
consequential. 'Afraid I already ate. Neil Baxter invited me
out.'

'So I understand.'

'He was called back in to take care of some problem,'
she added. 'I'd have thought someone else could have handled it.'

'Depends on the nature of the problem. It's his job to be
available when needed—especially with Conroy out of
town for the night. You realise he has an eye to the main
chance, of course?'

Green eyes sparked. 'Meaning, he asked me out with a
view to feathering his own nest? He's in no need of any
backing from me. He's already in line for the GM's job
when James Conroy decides he's had enough.'

'It isn't a foregone conclusion, by any means. He'll be
well aware of that. A word from the top at the right time
could swing it for him.'

It was what she had thought herself, but she wasn't about

to admit it. Ross hadn't moved from the chair, his whole attitude a spur to the anger building inside her.

'If you've finished, I'd like some privacy,' she said. 'You've no right to be here in *my* suite to start with!'

'I'll go when I'm good and ready,' he rejoined. 'One or two points we need to get straight. When I said we'd each live our own lives, I meant with some discretion. Swanning around with a member of staff can hardly be called that! The whole place was buzzing when I got back.'

'So what?' she demanded. 'Everyone knows the marriage is just a means to an end.'

'I don't give a damn what everyone knows!' Ross wasn't lounging any more, a dangerous spark in his eyes. 'Just take note.'

'Your precious pride suffering?' she asked scathingly. 'Means so much to a man, doesn't it? At least I didn't spend the whole afternoon...'

Ross hoisted a sardonic eyebrow as she broke off, biting her lip. 'Where exactly do you think I've been all afternoon?'

'Ten to one, with a woman,' she said, not about to back down again. 'Two nights' deprivation takes some making up for.'

Anger turned suddenly to amusement. 'Spoken with feeling! And there I was thinking I was being the true gallant giving you chance to catch up on your sleep last night.'

The wind taken completely out of her sails, Gina sought some pungent response. 'Don't flatter yourself!' was the best she could come up with, serving only to increase the amusement.

'Why try denying something that's so patently obvious? You were as ready as I was the other night, before the champagne caught up with you. As ready as you are now, in fact.'

'Of all the arrogant…' She caught herself up, realising how hackneyed she sounded, fury mounting as she met the grey eyes. 'I've no intention of providing you with entertainment of *any* kind from here-on-in!'

'Oh, I think you could be persuaded.'

Gina stood her ground as he came slowly, almost lazily to his feet, heart hammering against her ribcage, stomach muscles tensed. 'I'm telling you no!' she fired at him.

She may as well have held her tongue for all the notice he took. She struggled slightly as he slid his arms about her, but her heart wasn't in it. No part of her was in it.

His mouth was passionate. She found herself answering in the same vein, lips moving beneath his, parting to allow him access to the inner softness, her body moulding to his shape with abandonment.

She made no protest when he lifted her in his arms and bore her across to the bedroom, wanting him too desperately to care what she might reveal. There were lamps lit in here too, the beds already turned back by the maid. Ross laid her down on the nearest, stripping off his shirt before coming down alongside her to kiss her with mounting urgency.

She sought the buckle of his belt, easing the leather through the slot and sliding the zip to find him, while he removed her brief undergarment. They joined together in a frenzy, fired by the same surging, irresistible need.

It was some time before either of them could summon the energy to move after the tumultuous climax. Gina floated on a sea of satisfaction, mind blanked of everything outside of this moment.

'That went a whole lot faster than intended,' Ross murmured. He raised his head to look at her, scanning her face feature by feature, his smile slow. 'You're a hell of a woman, Gina Saxton!'

She was a hell of an idiot, letting this happen again, she thought wryly as reality intruded. She made a supreme effort to adopt the same easy, semi-teasing attitude, sliding a finger end across the firm lips.

'Must be the Harlow in me!'

Laughter sparkled his eyes. 'One thing you're certainly not is boring!'

'I do my best.' She stiffened in sudden realisation. 'You didn't use anything!'

'Didn't have time to think about it,' he admitted. His expression altered as he looked at her. 'I take it you're protected?'

Gina choked back the instinctive denial, closing heart and mind to the possible consequences. 'Of course.'

'That's OK, then.' He dropped a swift kiss on her lips, then rolled away from her to sit up. 'I'll be back. We've all night to come yet. The next couple of days, too, for that matter. We're going across to the island tomorrow. I've rented a house for the weekend.'

He was taking it for granted that she was as ready as he obviously was to take whatever pleasure was to be had from the affair, but she was past the point of no return. Whatever the eventual cost, it would be worth it, she told herself.

# CHAPTER SEVEN

IT WAS raining when they left the mainland, a warm, soft gentle rain that petered out as they passed beneath Lion's Gate Bridge. Mountains reared to either side of the Straight, white-capped and breathtaking. As they neared the island, the coastline broke into coves and inlets, and stretches of beach. Above and beyond lay the dark mass of forest.

They docked at Nanaimo, heading out onto the Island Highway running up the east coast in the car Ross had commandeered from the hotel. The scenery was magnificent, a wilderness barely touched by man.

'Have you been here before?' Gina asked, taking it all in.

'Once,' Ross acknowledged. 'Years ago.'

'Alone?'

'No.' His tone was easy. 'With a couple of college friends. We lived rough, camping out, fishing and hunting for food. Male bonding, it's called these days. Back then, it was just three guys with a yen to experience life in the raw for a while. Always meant to come back some time. Just never got round to it.'

Gina glanced his way, appraising the hard-edged profile outlined against the backcloth of forest; trying to visualise the younger image. She wished she could have known him then—except that she would have been about ten at the time he was speaking of.

The house he'd rented lay in a small private bay reached by a narrow dirt road. Built like an oversized log cabin, it overlooked the Straight, with superb views from the wide rear veranda to the mainland mountain ranges. Inside lay three *en suite* bedrooms, along with huge lounging and dining areas and a kitchen fitted with every aid to modern living.

'I left it to the agency to arrange a delivery,' said Ross when Gina opened the refrigerator door to discover it packed with food. 'They'll have tried to cover all tastes. There's a hot tub out back. Be a good place to share a nightcap, don't you think?'

'Can't think of a better,' she said, closing out any dissenting voices. 'Did you arrange all this yesterday?'

'Among other things.' He drew her to him, leaning his back against a work surface as he used both hands to smooth the hair back from her face, scrutinising every feature in much the same way he'd done the night before. The look in his eyes sent her pulse rate soaring. 'You're beautiful!'

'Hardly on a par with some I could mention,' she returned lightly, trying to stay on top of her emotions.

'If you're talking about the general LA line-up, you're streets ahead of most,' he said. 'You don't need to pile on the make-up to look good.'

His kiss was no let-down. She put everything she knew into answering it. They made love lying on a bearskin rug in front of a flaming log fire—both fakes, but realistic enough to add atmosphere. Confident in their isolation, Gina relinquished all inhibitions, answering every call made on her with a passion to match.

'Whoever it was that said all English women were frigid obviously chose the wrong samples,' Ross observed at one point, taking a moment or two to recover.

'Either that, or he was useless at it himself,' she returned, not really caring either way. 'That's something you'll never need to worry about.'

He laughed softly. 'Not this side of seventy, at any rate, I hope!'

'Only seventy?' she teased. 'Charlie Chaplin was still fathering babies in *his* seventies.'

She'd managed to forget about last night's neglect until now. The reminder of what it might possibly have achieved sent her spirits suddenly plunging. What she would do if it did happen, she couldn't begin to think.

Best not to go down that road at all unless forced, she told herself resolutely. It *was* only a chance.

Ross had made no reply to the sally. It was only when she turned her head to look at him that she realised he'd actually dozed off. She lay quietly studying the incisive features, feeling the warm, possessive weight of his hand at her breast. A month ago she hadn't even known he existed. From that to this was difficult to believe.

She was in love with him, she finally admitted. She'd fallen hook, line and sinker that very first week. Walking away then would have been hard, but nowhere near as hard as it was going to be when the time eventually came. The old saying about making one's bed and lying in it was more than apt.

But that wasn't now. Giving way to the need coursing through her again, she ran feather-light fingers down the arm stretched across her, and on down the length of his body, feeling muscle ripple beneath the taut, bronzed skin. His eyes opened as she found him, his response instant, the slow smile a stimulant in itself. Not that she needed any stimulation.

The afternoon was drawing to a close when they reluctantly decided enough was enough for the present. They took showers, then cooked steaks on the barbecue outside.

Gina made a salad and opened a bottle of wine, vowing to keep her own consumption to the one glass. She wanted to be in full awareness of every minute of this weekend together. For Ross it might just be sex; for her it was everything she had ever imagined lovemaking could be with the right person.

Apart from the occasional vessel passing through the Straight, there were few lights to be seen. Vancouver could be a million miles away. The night air was cool, but the hot tub more than compensated. Head back against the side-cushion, limbs relaxed in the delicious, bubbling warmth, memory on a back burner for the moment, Gina felt at peace with the world.

'I could stay here for ever,' she murmured dreamily.

'I know the feeling,' Ross rejoined. 'Life can be a bit too demanding at times.'

'It's what you wanted, though, isn't it?' she said. 'The company, I mean.'

'Sure,' he agreed. 'But it isn't everything. Oliver recognised that much himself—especially in the last few years. He took time out to be with my mother whenever he could. They did a lot of travelling together. Buena Vista isn't their only home. There are other properties in Barbados, and the Bahamas. I don't imagine she'll want to keep them on now though.'

'You wouldn't consider taking them over yourself?' Gina ventured.

'I might the Barbados one, if she has no objection. I had a hand in designing the place. You'd enjoy Barbados,' he added. 'It's a very laid-back island. Beautiful too. We could honeymoon there, if you like.'

She gave a brittle laugh. 'Oh, sure!'

'Why not?' he said. 'Don't you fancy a couple of weeks of this kind of thing?'

She looked at him in startled realisation. 'You're serious, aren't you?'

'Never more. We're going to need some rest and recuperation after the wedding, believe me. Not that I'd anticipate too much resting,' he added on a note that set the fires burning all over again.

Making love in a hot tub was an experience outside anything she could ever have imagined, though she doubted if it was new to Ross. Wrapped in the thick towelling robe he fetched from the house afterwards, wine glass in hand, his arm about her shoulders, she felt the closest she'd ever been to heaven. If only it could be like this for real, she thought yearningly.

'Have you seen anything of Roxanne since the will-reading?' she asked, bringing herself down to earth again.

'No,' he said. 'She's done a disappearing act.'

'Aren't you worried about her?'

Broad shoulders lifted. 'She can take care of herself.'

'What did she do to turn you against her?' Gina queried tentatively. 'Was it to do with money?'

Ross looked down at her, gaze sharpened. 'Has she approached you for any?'

'Yes,' she admitted. 'She needed to repay a loan.'

'You didn't give it to her?'

'The will had only just been read. I didn't have it *to* give. In any case...'

'In any case?' he prompted as she let the words trail away.

'It was rather a large amount.'

'*How* large?'

'Three hundred thousand.'

He said something harsh under his breath. 'I should have known!'

Gina would have happily left the whole subject alone at that point, but if Roxanne was to become her sister-in-law, for however short a time, it needed to be aired.

'Known what?' she asked.

'That she was still up to the same old tricks. She drove Gary into bankruptcy before leaving him. Ruined his life, *and* his health. I tried to warn him what she was like before he married her, but he wouldn't listen. He worshipped her.'

'Where is he now?' Gina ventured.

'Dead.' The tone was hard. 'He got into difficulties while swimming in the sea apparently. His body was never recovered.'

She drew in a breath. 'You don't think…'

'Who knows? Whichever way, he's gone. We were at Yale together.'

'He was here with you on that camping trip?'

'Yes.' Ross removed the arm from her shoulders, putting his glass down on the table. 'You called your parents yesterday, I take it?'

She shook her head, seeing impatience spring suddenly in his eyes.

'What are you waiting for?' he demanded.

'Courage,' she admitted. 'They're going to be badly hurt. Especially my mother. She's already feeling pushed out.'

'There's no reason why she should. Anyway, they have to know some time. It's Sunday tomorrow. A good day to find them both at home.'

He was right, of course. It was more than time she let them know what was going on. 'I'll do it first thing,' she promised.

'I'll make sure of it this time,' he said hardly. 'You're not backing out on me, Gina. There's too much at stake.'

'I've no intention of backing out,' she retorted, resenting his tone. 'Do you really think I'd turn down millions?'

Cynicism overtook impatience as he surveyed her. 'No, I guess not. Let's get to bed.'

It was on the tip of her tongue to tell him he'd be spend-

ing the night on his own, but that would be as much deprivation to her as to him. She was turning into the kind of
person she would have decried not so very long ago, she
acknowledged wryly.

She made the phone call straight after breakfast. Her father, it turned out, was playing golf, but her mother made
no secret of their disappointment in her for leaving it so
long to get in touch.

She received the news about the will badly enough. The
wedding plans left her too disturbed to speak at all for
several seconds.

'How can you possibly marry someone you only met
such a short time ago?' she got out. 'You can't even have
got to know him properly!'

She'd certainly got to know him improperly over the last
twenty-four hours, Gina reflected.

'I really do know what I'm doing, Mom,' she said, feeling a total fraud.

Ross took the receiver from her, startling her because
she hadn't realised he was that close.

'Hello, Mrs Saxton,' he said. 'I can understand how you
must be feeling, but I can assure you Gina is going to be
well taken care of. You've done a wonderful job bringing
her up. She's a credit to you. I'm looking forward to meeting you and your husband. My mother too. She'll be speaking to you herself shortly, to make arrangements.' He listened for a moment or two, expression unrevealing. 'That
really wouldn't be practical, I'm afraid.'

He handed the instrument back to Gina. 'She wants to
speak to you again.'

'I was saying that if you're going to be married at all, it
should be here,' her mother said. 'What did he mean by it
not being practical?'

Gina sought some diplomatic explanation. 'Just that

there'd be far too many people who wouldn't be able to make it,' she managed. 'A whole lot easier for you to come over here. You *will* come, won't you?' she added anxiously.

'As if we'd think of refusing.' Jean Saxton sounded resigned, though far from happy about it. 'It's going to be a shock for your father.'

'I know.' It was all Gina could say. 'I'll ring you again tomorrow.'

She replaced the receiver, hating herself. Hating Ross too at present.

'That's the rottenest thing I've ever done!' she burst out.

Ross slid his hands about her slender waist, drawing her closer to put his lips first to her temple then slowly down her cheek to probe the very tip of his tongue into the hollow just behind her earlobe, sending shivers chasing the length of her spine.

'Come on back to bed,' he said softly.

'Is sex all you can think about?' she accused, drawing a smile as he shifted his gaze from her flushed bare face under the tousled blonde hair down to the soft swelling curves revealed by the robe that had slipped back over her shoulders.

'Right now, yes,' he said.

They landed back in LA early on the Monday afternoon, driving straight to Buena Vista. Elinor welcomed them eagerly.

'The formal announcement went in on Saturday,' she said when they were seated on the terrace with drinks to hand. 'The media are already vying for exclusives.'

'No exclusives,' Ross declared with finality. 'Have you heard from Roxanne at all?'

'Not a word,' she confirmed. 'I've called the apartment

several times, but she's never in. Not that it's unusual, of course.'

'I'll take a run over and check,' he said. 'I've got the number of those friends of hers in Frisco somewhere, too. I can give them a try.'

'Any particular reason why you're so keen to get hold of her?' his mother asked.

'She wanted Gina to give her three hundred thousand to pay off a loan. I want to know who the debtor is.'

'I should never have mentioned it,' Gina said unhappily.

He shook his head. 'I'm glad you did. There's no way she could get her hands on that amount in a lump sum, so the debt must still be outstanding. Always providing she was telling you the truth to start with. She may just have been trying you out for a future soft touch.'

He got up again, leaving his drink untouched. 'I'll leave you two to talk weddings for now.'

Gina studied the glass in her hand as he headed back to the house, looking up to meet Elinor's smile.

'I'd say the weekend went well,'. she observed.

'Apart from breaking the news to my parents.'

'I was wondering when you were going to get round to it.' Elinor was hesitant, obviously only too aware of the difficulties. 'How did they take it?'

'Not very well,' Gina admitted. 'Although I've only spoken to my mother up to now.'

'It stands to reason it would be a shock for her, but I'm sure she'll come round. Perhaps I could call her myself?'

'Ross already spoke to her. I'm not sure whether it helped all that much, but they will be coming for the wedding.'

Elinor looked relieved. 'I'll speak to them later, then. They'll be staying here, of course. What about your partner?'

Gina had totally forgotten about Barbara until this moment. Another phone call she still had to make. 'She'll be too busy with the shop,' she said.

'Of course. Especially now she'll be running it on her own. Ross told me you were making over your share of the business to her.'

'I'm hardly going to be in need of it.' Gina gave a short laugh. 'I sometimes feel I'm living in fantasy land!'

'You'll adjust,' Elinor assured her. 'A year from now, you'll wonder how you lived any other kind of life.'

A year from now she may not even be here, Gina reflected. She didn't really see herself hanging around after the divorce went through. It was a hollow thought.

'I'm sorry for letting on about Roxanne wanting money,' she said, looking for a change of subject.

Elinor sighed and shrugged. 'It's nothing new, believe me. She probably borrowed on the strength of her expectations. I should have warned her that Oliver lost faith in her after Gary died. Gary was her husband.'

'I know. Ross told me.' Gina hesitated, not sure she should say any more than that. On the other hand, having it all in the open could save a lot of bitten lips. 'I suppose it was even harder for him to accept, Gary being such an old and close friend.'

'The only son of one of Oliver's oldest and closest friends too. Oliver blamed himself for giving her too much. She grew up expecting everything to be handed to her on a platter. Gary did his best to satisfy her, but it was never enough. She wouldn't even contemplate a baby. Not that she'd have been anything of a mother, I'm afraid.'

Elinor made a dismissive gesture reminiscent of her son's mannerism, briskening her tone. 'Enough of that. You and I have a lot to get through. Tomorrow, we go dress-hunting. I've already seen one or two I'd personally consider suitable, but you're the one who'll be wearing it. The invitations are ready to go out too. I thought you might like to look through the list.'

Gina shook her head. 'There's really no point. I shan't know anyone.'

'Ross must see to it that you meet some of them beforehand, then. Now, about the reception. I thought burgundy, cream and lemon would be a bit different for the colour scheme. Of course, you might have your own ideas?'

Gina shook her head, happy to just go along. If nothing else, the wedding had given Elinor something to occupy her mind at a time when she so badly needed it. The fact that it was all of it meaningless was something she herself just had to live with.

The media circus got under way without delay. PRINCE CHARMING TO WED HIS CINDERELLA blared one trite headline, HARLOW MAGNATES TO SEAL PARTNERSHIP FOR LIFE another. Gina grew rapidly weary of turning down the requests for interviews, for TV appearances; of dodging cameras wherever they went; of the sheer pressure of being in the public eye.

'Why are they making so much of it?' she asked Ross one morning after running a whole gauntlet of photographers outside the house. 'I know the Harlow name has a lot of standing, but they've the whole of Hollywood to go at for copy of the kind they're after, for heaven's sake!'

'As I told you before, the storyline *is* pure Hollywood,' he said. 'It will blow over. In the meantime, I'm afraid you'll just have to grin and bear it.'

They were in his office. Gina had called in on her way to attend a charity luncheon her future mother-in-law had arranged. Shirtsleeves rolled, he was leafing through a whole sheaf of literature concerning a South American property they were considering. Viewing the dark head, the hairline crisp against bronzed skin, she felt the familiar constriction in the pit of her stomach.

Drawn into the welter of wedding arrangements, she hadn't been able to spend much time here herself, and she'd seen little enough of him the past couple of weeks. They'd attended one or two functions, and she'd met a lot of people, but they hadn't spent a solitary night together since Vancouver.

Not that he'd have spent all his alone, she was certain.

'My parents arrive tomorrow,' she said. 'Are you going to be free to come with me to the airport?'

'Should be,' he agreed without looking up. 'I've a lunch appointment with Isabel, but nothing after that. Isabel Dantry,' he added, sensing the unspoken question. 'The investment banker? You'll be needing advice yourself once everything's settled. I'll have to introduce you.'

'I may not want to invest,' she said. 'We're not all into the must-have-more syndrome. The whole point of having money is to enjoy it, not just sit watching it grow!'

That did get a result. Ross studied her speculatively, taking in the spots of high colour on her cheekbones. 'Your genuine opinion, or just bloody-mindedness?'

'What would I have to be bloody-minded about?' she asked.

'You tell me,' he invited. 'You're obviously here for a purpose.'

'I came to ask you about the airport.'

'You could have done that on the phone.'

'So maybe I'm just sick and tired of this whole fiasco!' she burst out, giving way to the emotions that had been eating into her for days. 'Maybe I'm regretting ever agreeing to it in the first place!'

'Too late.' His tone was deceptively mild. 'You burned your bridges when you gave the go-ahead.'

She'd burned a whole lot more in allowing herself to fall for him, she thought bitterly. All she was to him was a means to an end.

'Bear up,' he said. 'In four days we'll be in Barbados with it all behind us. The house has its own private beach. We can swim in the nude, make love under the stars. Sound good?'

'Idyllic.' She looked at her watch. 'I'd better be on my way.'

'How's my mother getting there?' he asked as she rose to her feet.

'Michael is driving her in. I'm using the Cadillac.' She kept her tone level. 'Time I got to grips with the system.'

'Sure.' His attention was already drifting back to the file still in his hand. 'I'll see you tomorrow, then.'

Penny had been missing when Gina had arrived, but she was at her desk now. She looked up with a smile.

'Hi! How's it all going?'

Gina forced a smile in return. 'Swimmingly! How are you?'

'Wonderful! Just coming up to the twelfth week!'

Until this moment, Gina had totally forgotten the other woman was pregnant. She made an appropriate response, unable to deny a certain envy. Penny had a real marriage, a good marriage—the kind she'd always imagined for herself.

The fear that *she* might be pregnant had proved groundless, for which she could only be thankful. She was on the Pill now, though it wasn't going to be necessary because she wouldn't be sleeping with Ross again under any circumstances. She'd had enough of being used.

# CHAPTER EIGHT

THE Saxtons arrived on an early-evening flight from Heathrow looking typically travel-weary after the long haul. They greeted Ross with reservation.

'I have to say, it's not the way we'd have preferred,' Leslie Saxton declared, 'but Gina is old enough to make her own decisions. All we ask is that you take care of her. She's very precious to us.'

'She's very precious to me too,' Ross assured him.

True enough, considering what he stood to lose without her, the she in question thought hardly.

'Will you stop talking about me as if I'm not here!' she exclaimed, summoning a laugh. 'We'd better get out to the car before Michael gets moved on.'

'Michael?' her mother queried.

'Elinor's chauffeur. She's really eager to see you both.'

The two of them were quiet on the journey. Gina had a very good idea how they were feeling. She'd been more than a bit overwhelmed by it all herself on arrival. She was still in many ways.

She cast a swift glance at the man occupying the other pull-down seat, pulses quickening as always to the impact of his dark good looks. There was no turning off the physical attraction, but her resolution remained strong. He was in for a rude awakening.

Elinor was warm and welcoming without gushing. She left it to Gina to show the newcomers to the bedroom they'd be occupying for the length of their stay, inviting them back down for a light supper when they'd sorted themselves out a little.

'I can see why you wouldn't want to give all this up,' Jean Saxton observed on the way to the room. 'It's a whole different world. But why rush into marriage the way you're doing?'

Gina had only told them she'd been left the shares, not the rest, but they were going to find out sooner or later.

'Oliver made it a condition that Ross and I married,' she said, bracing herself for the inevitable reaction.

Jean stopped in mid-step, her pleasantly featured face expressing a multitude of emotions. 'You mean you don't even have any feelings for him?'

'I didn't say that.' Gina did her best to sound positive. 'It's simply happening sooner than it might have done in normal circumstances.'

'But it isn't exactly a love match?'

'Not in the accepted sense, perhaps.'

'What other sense is there?' Jean sounded disturbed. 'You've changed since you came here, Gina. There's a hardness in you that was never there before.'

'It's called self-confidence,' she returned lightly. 'Something you have to develop to survive in this neck of the woods. You don't have to worry about me, Mom. I really do know what I'm doing.'

'You said that before, and I didn't believe it then,' Jean rejoined. 'I know you're not our own flesh and blood, but we love you, Gina. Of course we're going to worry!'

'I think we'd better move on,' Leslie put in diplomatically. 'We can talk later.'

Gina saw them to the bedroom, closing the door on them feeling thoroughly ashamed. She was still deceiving them. Elinor too.

Ross was seated out on the terrace alone. He regarded her shrewdly as she joined him. 'Trouble?'

'I told them about the condition,' she said. 'They're far from over the moon about it.'

'Maybe you should have left them in happy ignorance, then.'

'And have someone else fill them in? Not that they were happy about it anyway.'

Ross surveyed her for a moment, brows drawn. 'And how do you feel?'

'Oh, ecstatic!' She made no attempt to downplay the irony. 'I'm going to be a millionairess. What could be better than that?'

'If you're thinking about backing out again, you can forget it,' he said on a harder note. 'We've come this far, we'll go the rest. What brought this mood on anyway? You were fine about it until yesterday.'

She'd been fine until he left her to stew for two weeks, she could have told him, but that would be giving too much away.

'I'd convinced myself that money made up for everything else we're missing,' she lied. 'I was wrong.'

'I wouldn't say we're missing all that much,' he rejoined.

'You mean the sex?' She lifted her shoulders, fighting to maintain control. 'You can get that anywhere. So can I, if it comes to that. Oh, I'll go through with it, don't worry. I've got too used to the good life to turn it down on a point of principle. Did you manage to trace Roxanne?'

He accepted the sudden switch without comment, face expressionless. 'She's in Phoenix. Been there some weeks apparently, with some man she met in Frisco.'

'She'll be at the wedding?'

'I didn't get to speak to her. The man she's living with said she was resting and didn't want to be disturbed. He's to pass on the message. What she does about it is entirely up to her.'

He got to his feet as her parents emerged from the house along with his mother, tone easy again. 'How about a drink before we eat? I always find it a good way to wind down after a long flight.'

The evening was long, conversation stilted. Gina couldn't blame her parents for feeling the way they did. She should have told them everything from the beginning, she acknowledged ruefully. It would at least have given them time to come to some kind of terms.

Elinor made every effort to keep things going, but it was a losing battle. Jean broke the party up at ten, claiming she could hardly keep her eyes open.

'I think I'll have an early night myself,' Elinor said when the Saxtons had departed. 'There are things I have to catch up on.'

'Do you need any help?' Gina offered, reluctant to be left alone with Ross.

The other shook her head. 'Nothing to do with the wedding. That's all in hand now. Don't make a noise when you leave,' she told her son. 'You know how sound carries at night up here. We've a full programme planned for tomorrow.'

'I'll watch it,' he promised. 'I shan't be long, anyway. I've a heavy day tomorrow too.'

Gina picked up her wine glass and drained it as Elinor departed, putting it down again with a thud. 'I think I'll do the same,' she said.

'Not yet.' Ross spoke quietly but with purpose. 'We need to talk.'

'I said all I needed to say earlier,' she returned. 'Wrong time, wrong place, if it's sex you've got in mind.'

The spark that sprang in the grey eyes was pulse-jerking.

'If it was, we wouldn't be sitting here. Sorry if I haven't been dancing attendance as much as you'd like this past week or two. I've been pretty tied up.'

She didn't doubt it. The question was, with whom?

'Just how long will we have to stay married?' she asked, keeping a tight rein on her tongue.

The expression that crossed the lean features was come and gone too fast for analysis. 'A few months, maybe.'

'It's *that* easy to get divorced over here?'

'It can be, providing both parties are in agreement.'

'Maybe you should have me sign a pre-nuptial agreement,' she said. 'After all, you'll still be worth a lot more than I will.'

His lips twisted. 'If you're going to keep this up, I'll leave you to that early night.'

Gina got up with him, steeling herself not to weaken. 'Will you be here tomorrow?'

'My best man's due in from Vegas at five,' he said. 'We might make it for dinner. Otherwise, I'll see you in church.'

He made no attempt to kiss her, unsurprisingly, just turned and went. Gina stood for several minutes where he'd left her, wishing her grandfather had left well alone. Discounting the mistake she'd made over the business, she'd been happy enough in her old life. She'd certainly have been a whole lot better off never knowing Ross existed.

While never fully relaxing her guard, Jean loosened up a little over the course of a day spent touring the city. She and Leslie had been living and working in Bakersfield at the time of the adoption, so LA wasn't exactly new territory, though they found it strange after twenty-five years in a totally different environment.

Back at the house by four, Gina took advantage of the

afternoon sun to chill out for an hour down at the pool, needing to be alone for a while.

This time tomorrow she would be on her way to the church. One of the city's grandest, naturally. Every bride was supposed to dream of her big day, where she'd be the centre of attention, but not every bride was called on to face the degree of attention she was going to be undergoing tomorrow. And for what? A marriage already scheduled to end. She could make Ross pay dearly by refusing to agree to the divorce, of course, but what was the use?

Elinor came to join her, looking a little concerned. 'You've been so quiet all day,' she said. 'Are you OK?'

'Just a bit tired,' Gina claimed. 'I didn't get much sleep last night.'

'You'll probably get even less tonight,' Elinor observed. 'I didn't sleep at all the night before I married Oliver. I'm so glad he found you again. Not just for his sake, but for mine and Ross's too. I'm gaining a daughter, Ross the kind of wife I always hoped he'd have some day. Apart from having Oliver here with us, I couldn't be happier than I am right now.'

Gina murmured some response, feeling lower than ever. Elinor might be living in cloud cuckoo land where the marriage was concerned, but she was such a genuine person. She deserved so much better than this.

She went up to shower and dress for the evening at six, coming down to find Ross had arrived with his best man, Brady Leeson. She already knew Brady had been the third man on the Vancouver Island venture. Ruggedly attractive beneath a shock of bright copper hair, he greeted her with frank admiration.

'The description didn't do you justice,' he said.

He would know the reason for the marriage, Gina assumed, wondering just what the description had been.

Whether Ross would have told him all of it was open to doubt. She avoided looking at the latter directly, though she could feel his gaze on her. He was still angry with her; she could feel that too. He was going to be angrier still tomorrow night—for what good it would do him.

The two of them left again soon after dinner. Not to take advantage of an early night, Gina suspected. She went up herself at ten, leaving her parents to Elinor.

She expected to be awake half the night worrying about all she had to face the next day, but she slept right through till seven. Mental exhaustion, she reckoned. The morning passed with excruciating slowness. She ate lunch only because both her mother and Elinor insisted she have something on her stomach to see her through until the reception. Five o'clock in the afternoon seemed a strange time to hold a wedding, but it was quite the done thing here.

She'd already met the twins who were to be her brides-maids. They arrived at one, along with the hairdresser and beautician. Outnumbered, Leslie made himself scarce until it was time to don his own wedding outfit.

Elinor, Jean and the bridesmaids left the house at four in a white stretch limousine. Gina and her father were to travel in a vintage Rolls-Royce, which would also carry her and Ross to the reception.

Watching her descend the stairs in the lovely, classically styled white gown, Leslie blinked hard on the moisture gathering in the corners of his eyes. 'You look so beautiful,' he said. 'We're going to miss you!'

'I'm going to miss you too,' she said truthfully, despising herself for doing this to them. 'But it isn't as if we're never going to see one another again. I'll come over as often as I can.'

If Leslie noticed that she said 'I' rather than 'we', he didn't comment on it.

The Rolls drew a lot of attention on the journey down-town. Gina had anticipated some media attention, but was totally unprepared for the crowds of watchers gathered be-hind rope barriers outside the church, for the banks of cam-eras, the television crews. Flash bulbs almost blinded her as she traversed the red carpet spread across the pavement. It took everything she had to keep a smile on her face. The bride must at least *look* blissful.

It was something of a relief to gain the shelter of the church entrance, where the twins in their garnet dresses awaited her, but it was only the start. Packed rows of faces all turned her way as they started down the aisle to the strains of the 'Canon in D' by Johann Pachelbel.

Standing at the aisle end of the third row from the front, sapphire eyes glittering beneath her wide-brimmed cream hat, Dione Richards was only too recognisable. Gina doubted if Elinor would have added her name to the guest list, considering recent associations, which meant Ross must have. But then, why not? The congregation was prob-ably peppered with his conquests.

Looking superb in a dark blue tuxedo, he awaited her coming at the foot of the red-carpeted steps leading to the altar proper. Gina felt her throat contract as she met his eyes, her chest go tight as a drum.

'I see you put your hair up,' he murmured with an ironic tilt to his lips as she took her place by his side.

'I thought the occasion warranted it this time,' she said.

Time moved in a series of impressions after that: the solemnity of the service; signing the register; walking back down the aisle on the arm of the man now her husband, narrowly suppressing the urge to blow a kiss to Dione; facing the mêlée outside again.

'Thank God that's over!' Ross exclaimed in the car tak-ing the two of them on to the reception. He studied her face, making no attempt to touch her. 'You look wonderful!'

'I feel like an exhibit,' she said. Conscious of the lack of a screen between them and the chauffeur, she made an effort to lighten both tone and expression. 'I didn't expect quite so many people out there.'

'Weddings are a draw any day of the week,' Ross returned. 'We still have the reception to get through, so don't start relaxing yet.' The pause was meaningful. 'We'll have plenty of time for that this next couple of weeks. I cleared the decks as far as possible, so there shouldn't be any problem.'

Only the one he'd still to learn of, she thought. They were due to spend tonight at the apartment, flying out to Barbados in the morning. She looked forward to seeing his expression when he realised the honeymoon he'd cleared the decks for was going to be a non-event.

It wasn't far to the hotel. Yet another phalanx of photographers awaited their arrival. Elinor and her parents, along with the best man and bridesmaids, had already formed the welcoming line-up in readiness for the guests even now beginning to arrive. Taking her place at Ross's side, Gina geared herself up for yet another ordeal.

It took an age. Her hand felt crushed from all the shaking, her face stiff from keeping the smile going brightly. She'd met some of them already, but hadn't retained any names. She felt like throwing her arms round Meryl Thornton in sheer relief.

'We must get together again,' Meryl said. 'I'll give you a call when you get back.'

'Do,' Gina urged.

Her enthusiasm faded as the next in line moved into view. The beautiful, superbly dressed brunette wore a smile that left her eyes devoid of any hint of warmth.

'Congratulations,' Dione said in a silky purr, not bothering to extend a hand. She turned her attention immediately to Ross, the smile altering in character. 'You're a lucky man. She's really quite lovely!'

'Isn't she?' he agreed. 'Glad you could make it, Dione.'

'As if I could possibly miss *such* an occasion!' she said with deliberated extravagance.

She went on her way, trailing the man she was with, leaving Gina gritting her teeth. The knowledge that Ross had slept with the woman—and was more than likely sleeping with her still—was impossible to just ignore.

'Bear up,' he murmured. 'It's almost the end of the line.'

From the superb ice carvings decorating each and every table, through an equally superb five-course meal to the accompaniment of music played by a top-line quartet, the reception was exquisitely presented. Both bridegroom and best man did their duty with speeches that drew laughter and applause, while Leslie produced a short but well-thought-out piece that made Gina want to cry.

There was dancing after they finished eating, started off by the bridal pair themselves in accordance with tradition.

'Another half an hour, and we'll leave them to it,' Ross said on the floor. He kissed her, smiling drily at the applause that greeted the gesture. 'I think we can be said to have given it our best shot.'

Gina made no reply. Unprepared for it—although she should have been—the kiss had disturbed her carefully nurtured objectivity. The feel of him, lean and hard against her, undermined her even further.

'I notice Roxanne didn't bother to turn up,' she said, desperate for something to take her mind off bodily urges she couldn't control. 'Haven't you even heard from her?'

'Not a word.'

He sounded indifferent, but he had to feel *something*, she

thought. No matter what she'd done, Roxanne was his only sibling. He couldn't just disown her altogether.

'Your mother must be hurt,' she said.

'She's been that too many times to expect much else.'

'Surely if you talked to her. Really talked to her, I mean.'

'Unless it's attached to an offer of money, talking's useless. I'd have thought you'd recognised that much for yourself.'

The slow movement of the body so close to hers was robbing her of the ability to think clearly about anything but just that. She ached in every fibre with the need to be closer still, to be part of him again. It was going to take every ounce of will-power she had to do what she planned on doing.

So don't, whispered a small voice at the back of her mind.

A man she couldn't for the life of her remember receiving earlier tapped Ross on the shoulder. 'Time you gave the rest of us poor slobs a chance,' he grinned.

Laughing, Ross relinquished her into the other arms. 'Just don't take any advantages,' he warned.

Gina pasted the smile back on her face as the newcomer swung her into motion again, aware of the watching eyes. So much for getting away!

Others joined in, crowding the dance floor to the extent that it was impossible to do little more than sway in time to the music. Someone else claimed her, then someone else again. She did her best to keep up a light conversation with them all. It was all part and parcel of the occasion. Something she just had to bear with. Inwardly, she was still grappling with the temptation to abandon everything and just go with the flow.

It took the glimpse through the crowd of Dione in Ross's arms to bring the battle to an abrupt end. They looked what they were: two people on intimate terms with each other. The fury sweeping through her was all-consuming. He could at least have left the damned woman alone on this of all occasions—if only for the look of it!

She put up a pretence of enjoying herself far too much to leave when he did come to find her some half an hour later.

'Have another glass of champagne!' she invited, fishing a bottle from the ice bucket by the table where she was sitting with the Thorntons and others. 'The night is still young!'

Ross eyed her quizzically. 'How many have you had?'

With no intention of allowing alcohol to ruin her plan of attack, she'd stuck to the bare minimum, but she wasn't about to admit it. 'I lost count,' she said airily. 'Does it matter? I'm not driving.'

'We've a five-hour flight in the morning,' he returned. 'You're going to be tired.'

One of the men at the table said something low-toned to his neighbour, drawing a grin. Ross ignored the pair of them. 'It's midnight already.'

'The witching hour!' she exclaimed. 'That surely calls for another drink! A last dance, then,' as he shook his head. 'Listen, they're playing our song!'

There was a deep-down spark in the grey eyes, though his expression remained easy. He put out a hand. 'So they are.'

The quartet were playing a number she didn't even recognise. Ross drew her close, his hands hard at her waist. Her eyes were on a level with his mouth; she could feel his breath on her cheek, cool and fresh.

'Game still on, then,' he said softly.

'If that's what you want to call it,' she rejoined. 'Smile,

darling, we're under surveillance! You wouldn't want to give the media the wrong impression, would you?'

'The media weren't admitted,' he said. 'What was it you said once about a floor show?'

She gave a laugh. 'Bridegroom arrested for wife-beating at wedding reception. That would definitely make the headlines!'

His jaw tautened. 'Cut it out!'

'Sure.' She used the word with deliberation. 'My lips are sealed!'

'Why?' he asked after a moment.

'You know why,' she said, abandoning the act. 'What's the point in making out this is anything but a means to get our hands on the shares my grandfather left? I'll live with you because I don't want the Harlow name made a total mockery of, but I won't sleep with you again.'

The hands at her back had hardened still further. 'Is that a fact?'

'You can bet on it,' she said. 'I'll be occupying the guest room tonight.'

He held her a little away from him to look into her vibrant face beneath the sparkling diamond tiara Elinor had talked her into having, mouth dangerously set. 'I wouldn't count on it.'

'Oh, I doubt if you'd resort to force!'

'I don't intend to,' he said. 'You're no ice maiden, Gina. We already proved that.'

'Things can change.' There was a hard knot in her throat, another in her chest, but she wasn't about to go under. 'You don't need me to prove your virility. There's a more than adequate supply of willing partners out there. In here too, if it comes to that. Dione Richards, for instance. The two of you looked very cosy!'

There was derision in his eyes now. 'Cosy is the last

word I'd apply to Dione. She doesn't have any bearing on the situation anyway. We've some sorting out to do.'

It had to come eventually, Gina acknowledged. They may as well get it over with.

'I'm ready when you are,' she said.

She drew her first deep breath as he led her off the floor again, aware of the weakness in her limbs. She'd amazed herself these last few minutes; she'd certainly given Ross a shock. He wasn't going to get through her guard, whatever pressure he brought to bear. It was time he realised that she had a will just as strong as his when it came to the test.

It was only when taking her leave of her parents that she realised she wouldn't be seeing them again. They were flying home the day after tomorrow—no, actually tomorrow, considering it was already gone twelve.

'I'll call you from Barbados,' she promised, wondering what she would tell them. She could always fall back on describing the scenery and the weather, she supposed. They'd hardly expect any more intimate details.

Elinor gave both her and Ross warm hugs. 'See you when you get back,' she said.

Gina avoided looking at her mother, knowing how she must feel hearing that. She loved both the Saxtons very much, and always would, but there was no denying that things could never be quite the same.

Michael was waiting to drive the three of them back to the house. Ross had ordered a cab. It was coming up to two by the time they reached the Beverly Harlow.

He'd said nothing in the cab, and said nothing on the way up to the apartment. Waiting while he unlocked the outer door, Gina was totally unprepared for his sudden move to sweep her up and carry her over the threshold.

'That's one tradition out of the way,' he said tautly. 'One more to go!'

She struggled as he bore her through to the main bedroom, but it made no impression on him. He dropped her on the Empire-sized bed, keeping her down with a hand on her shoulder. Her dress fastened down the front with tiny pearl buttons to waist-level. Gina caught at his hand as he began to unfasten them.

'Don't you damn well dare!' she said through her teeth. 'I told you it's no go!'

He gave a short laugh. 'We'll see, shall we?'

She twisted her head away as he came down over her, but she couldn't escape his mouth. If the kiss had been forceful she could have held on to the fury driving her, but his lips were almost gentle, brushing, teasing, playing with the soft fullness, his tongue a silky caress.

She could do nothing to curb the heat and hunger spreading through her. Her lips parted, allowing him access, her body abandoning one kind of tension to gain another. Her hands lifted to the dark head, fingers plunging into the crisp thickness of his hair, the past days wiped from mind by the emotional storm consuming her.

The buttons popped with a faint pinging sound as he ran a hand down behind the bodice of the dress. Gina didn't care about the ruination, didn't care about anything but making up for the deprivation she'd suffered. Ross reached behind her to lower the long zip, easing the whole dress down over her hips to drop it in a silken pile on the floor.

She was wearing little beneath, her stockings garter-topped, her panties and bra mere wisps of white lace. He left the stockings on, coming down again to put his lips to each peaking, tingling nipple in turn, dragging moans from her aching throat at the exquisite sensation.

He moved on slowly, tantalising her quivering flesh with

tiny kisses, nuzzling her waist, her hipbone, lingering for
eternity on the fluttering skin just above the triangle of
blonde hair before sliding lower still to penetrate the very
centre of her being. Back arched, lips parted on a silent
scream, Gina was lost to everything but that flickering
flame, shudder after shudder running through her as she
climaxed.

She made a soft sound of protest when he lifted himself
away from her, but it was only to rid himself of his own
clothing. She needed no further stimulus, and he offered
none, each powerful thrust of his loins a token of his mas-
tery, carrying her through to an overwhelming finale.

It took him a moment or two to recover enough strength
to lift himself away from her. Gina lay motionless as he
got up. He'd made his point. She was incapable of saying
no to him and meaning it.

She watched him as he headed for the bathroom, even
now feeling a stirring inside at the mere sight of the leanly
muscled back and firm masculine behind. Where they went
from here she wasn't sure. She'd goaded him into what had
just happened; she might also have called time on whatever
feelings he did have for her.

She'd pulled herself together enough to have got up and
donned a negligee by the time Ross emerged from the bathroom. He was wearing a towelling robe similar to the one
in the guest suite. From the look of his hair, he'd stuck his
head under the shower. To cool off, she imagined.

'We need to talk,' he said before she could open her
mouth. Not that she had any idea what to say anyway.
'Properly, I mean. No more point-scoring.' His regard was
dispassionate. 'Agreed?'

'Agreed,' she said low-toned.

'We both of us knew what we were getting into when
this started,' he continued. 'The physical attraction was a

bonus. It can be still if you stop trying to make me out to be the bad guy.'

'You mean accept you the way you are, or do the other thing,' she retorted.

'There you go again!' Exasperation drew a line between his brows. 'I mean we should take advantage of the situation and get the most out of the relationship. We're good together. I'd say we just proved that.'

'What we just proved,' she said wryly, 'is that I'm weak in the won't department.'

A smile touched his lips. 'You think I'd have forced you if you hadn't given in?'

She shook her head. 'You wouldn't demean yourself.'

'Glad you realise it.' He waited a moment in anticipation of some further comment from her. 'So?'

'So, I think you're right, and we should make the best of things,' she said, smothering her deeper emotions.

'Apology accepted.' He laughed as her eyes sparked. 'I guess I asked for it to a great extent.'

There was a pause. Once again Ross was the one to break it. 'How do you feel about cementing the pact in time-honoured fashion?'

'I thought we just did,' she said.

'Call it a preliminary bout. Main event still to come.'

With her insides already melting, Gina let go of the last remnants of self-preservation, rewarded by the flare in his eyes as she let the negligee fall to the ground. At least he still wanted her.

## CHAPTER NINE

BARBADOS was a dream island, the villa a delight. Open-plan for the most part, with acres of coolly tiled floor, the decor was pure Caribbean. Gina loved it on sight.

The maid service she would happily have done without, though Ross appeared to have no objection. They spent the first couple of days on the private beach, swimming when they felt like it, sunbathing with proper caution and generally chilling out. Lovemaking was left for the moonlit, star-spangled nights.

They toured the island in one of the open-sided, soft-topped Jeeps, passing through fields of swaying sugar cane where workers paused in their toil to wave a cheerful greeting. Gina much enjoyed the Barbadian dialect, although finding it difficult sometimes to derive a meaning. The phrase 'I ain't no bride', overheard spoken by one man to another, left her totally baffled until Ross explained it simply meant the speaker was no model of good behaviour, and had nothing whatsoever to do with the marital state.

The first ripple in the sea came when they had lunch at one of the island's top hotels one day. Gina had noted the way a woman seated alone at a table on the far side of the restaurant kept eyeing them, but didn't expect to return from a visit to the bathroom to find the attractive redhead now seated at their table in conversation with Ross.

'Hi there!' she greeted, still laughing over some remark he'd apparently just made. 'I'm Samantha Barton. Ross tells me you're on your honeymoon. I wouldn't have come over if I'd known that.'

'Sam lives here,' Ross explained. 'She has a design studio on Broad Street. I didn't see her when we came in.'

'I moved here to escape the LA rat race a couple of years ago,' Samantha tagged on. 'Never looked back. What do you think of the island?'

'It's beautiful,' Gina acknowledged, putting on a sociable front. 'I could live here myself.'

'Especially in the Harlow villa! I had the use of it for a few weeks until I got myself sorted out.'

'You're a friend of the family, then?' Gina hazarded.

'More an acquaintance. I've done some design work at Buena Vista. Ross arranged for me to use the villa.' She turned her attention back his way, her smile a little too intimate for Gina's comfort. 'I was very grateful.'

Gina made a mental note to check whether Ross had visited the island himself a couple of years ago, pulling herself up sharply on the realisation that she was falling into the same old trap. Judging from the woman's looks and air of familiarity, it was on the cards that there had been some interaction between the two of them in the past, but even if the marriage had been real, his life prior to their own meeting would have been his affair, not hers.

Samantha was here at the hotel to advise on the restaurant redecoration, it appeared. She had a house up the west coast near Speightstown.

'I'm having a bit of a soirée tonight,' she said casually on preparing to leave at last. 'I'd love the two of you to come.'

'We'll be there,' Ross promised before Gina could think up an adequate reason why not.

'Great! Eight onwards, then.' She gave Gina a look that held just a hint of triumph. 'Look forward to seeing you.'

'You don't seem too enthused,' Ross observed in the silence that followed her departure.

Gina summoned a smile, a light rejoinder. 'I'm not all that bothered about meeting a load of people we're never likely to see again.'

'We've had a week on our own,' he said. 'I'd have thought you'd be ready for some company.'

'Meaning, you are?' she asked.

'I guess I am, yes,' he said. 'For a few hours, at any rate.'

She kept the smile going. 'That's fine, then.'

The subject wasn't mentioned for the rest of the afternoon. They took a boat out and spent an enjoyable three hours touring the coastline. Gina had meant it when she'd said she could live there herself. Compared with LA, the island was an oasis of peace and laid-back tranquillity.

It was late when they got back to the villa. There was just time to grab a bite to eat before dressing for the evening affair. With Samantha close to Ross in age, Gina chose to emphasise her comparative youth with a bias-cut dress designed to show off her figure to its best advantage. Fitted to mid-thigh from a wide, boat-shaped neckline that left her shoulders almost bare and offered a tantalising glimpse of softer flesh, it flared just enough to draw attention to the length of leg left exposed. A pair of spindle-heeled sandals made the latter look even longer.

Not bad, she thought critically, viewing her reflection. On impulse, she swept her hair up, leaving little tendrils to curl into her nape and about her face. Smoothed with just a hint of shadow, lashes darkened by mascara, her eyes were vivid against her tanned skin.

Emerging from the *en suite* bathroom, the briefest of towels slung about lean hips, Ross gave a low whistle. 'That,' he exclaimed, 'is a sight to perk any man up!'

'I didn't realise you needed perking up,' she said.

He laughed. 'A figure of speech, I think you'd call it. You look fantastic, anyway!'

There was a moment when he seemed about to make some other observation, then he moved to the bed, where his clothes for the evening were ready laid out, and began to dress.

Gina had hoped he was going to suggest they stayed home instead of going to this party. She would willingly have sacrificed all the effort she'd put into her appearance. As it obviously wasn't to be, she just had to make the best of it.

Striking himself in dark brown trousers and shirt, along with a cream jacket, Ross kept a casual conversation going as they headed along the coast. Gina made every effort to respond in the same vein, hauling herself over the coals for allowing herself to be dragged down again. So what if he and Samantha had had something going in the past? It wasn't to say he still harboured a desire for her.

She was clutching at straws, and she knew it. The way the two of them had been looking at one another when she first saw them together, there was certainly something there.

The house at the romantically named Cobblers Cove was about the same size as the Harlow residence. Built to a similar, open-plan design, and superbly furnished, it was already teeming with people when they got there. So much for the 'bit of a soirée', Gina thought drily.

Eye-catching in gold, Samantha greeted the pair of them like guests of honour. It was obvious from the start that most people there knew who they were. Obvious, too, that it was a moneyed crowd. Samantha must be doing very well indeed to move in such circles, Gina reflected.

She certainly lost little time in separating the two of them, leaving her in the company of an older, distinguished-looking man called Adrian, while she dragged

Ross off to meet someone who was in the hotel business here on the island, and looking to sell. Gina could have claimed that it was as much of interest to her to meet this person, considering her shares in the company, but Ross made no attempt to say it, and she wasn't about to kick him in the teeth in front of everyone.

'I'm surprised Ross would be willing to share you, looking the way you do,' Adrian declared. 'I certainly wouldn't!'

'Have you known Samantha long?' Gina asked, taking the gambit no more seriously than it was meant.

'Just over a year,' he said. 'We live together.' He read the unspoken question in her swift glance, his smile untroubled. 'I'm forty-six. Not that much more than the difference between you and your husband, I'd say. What's in a few years, anyway?'

What indeed? she thought, relieved that Samantha had a man of her own in tow. A ridiculous reaction, she had to admit.

'Is the house yours?' she asked.

'It is. Had it built last year. The interior decor's all down to Sam though. She's a clever lady.' The pause was brief. 'She tells me she and your husband are old friends. I sense a bit more than that.'

Gina steeled herself to show no emotion. 'Would you be bothered if there had been more?'

His shrug was philosophical. 'What happened before we met isn't important. All I ask is faithfulness while we're together. I dare say you feel the same way.'

She might feel it, she could have told him, there was a fat chance of it happening. 'I hadn't really thought about it,' she prevaricated. 'I suppose I just take it for granted.'

'Take nothing for granted,' he warned. 'There is a lot of temptation out there. I'm not immune to it myself—especially right now.' The last with a smile that robbed the words of any ulterior motive. 'You're a very lovely young woman, Gina. A man would have to be insensible not to be aware of it.

'Having said that, it's maybe the wrong moment to ask if you'd like to see the gardens,' he added on a humorous note. 'I'm in need of a breath of fresh air after all this conditioned stuff.'

There was no sign of Ross and Samantha in the immediate vicinity. Gina forced herself to concentrate on the man in front of her. 'I'd love to see the gardens. I could do with a breather myself.'

People had already spilled out onto the spacious stone-paved patio, some dancing on an oval floor which appeared to be covering a pool below, music provided by a trio. Gina caught a glimpse of the sea through the trees backing the patio, shining silver in the moonlight.

The gardens lay to either side and the front of the house. Subtly lit, they were the best Gina had ever seen. Myriad scents assailed her nostrils.

'It's wonderful,' she told Adrian with sincerity. 'I'd love a garden like this, only we have an apartment.'

'So move to a house,' he said, as if it were the simplest thing in the world. 'Or have one built to your own specification. An apartment's no place to have children. Assuming you plan to have children.'

'Of course.' Gina kept the smile going with an effort. 'Not just yet though. I'm still getting used to being married.'

'I wouldn't wait too long,' he advised. 'My wife and I might still be together if we'd started a family.'

If a marriage had to rely on children to keep it going, it wasn't worth much to start with, she thought.

They returned to the patio via a path that brought them

out to the rear, just in time to see Samantha and Ross emerge from another path leading into the trees.

There was nothing to be read from either face. Samantha was the first to speak, her tone blithe.

'I've been showing Ross the new boat. He thinks he may go for one himself if he decides to keep the house on. Where did you two get to?'

'I've been showing Gina the gardens.' Adrian sounded easy enough on the surface, though Gina thought she detected a certain wariness. The two of them had been missing nearly an hour. Time enough for anything.

'How did the meeting go?' she asked with some deliberation. 'Is the hotel a viable proposition?'

'Not for Harlows,' Ross answered smoothly. 'Why don't we have a dance as we're out here?'

A curt refusal trembled on her lips, bitten back with some difficulty. She accompanied him onto the floor in silence, unable to stop herself from stiffening when he put his arms about her.

'Something bothering you?' he asked.

'What makes you think anything is bothering me?' she countered.

'Because I may as well be holding a stick of celery. I realise you weren't too keen on coming, but you looked happy enough a few minutes ago with Adrian.'

'I was,' she said. 'He's a very nice man. Attractive too, for his age. Samantha's done well for herself.'

'Yes, she has. So has he. They make a good pair.'

'Better than the two of you did?' The words were out before she could stop them this time, instantly regretted.

It was a moment or two before Ross answered. When he did speak it was with measured tones. 'Is this what I can expect every time you meet a woman I'm already acquainted with?'

'No, of course not.' She did her best to achieve the right note. 'We're *both* of us completely free agents. So, are you really considering keeping the villa on?'

An indefinable expression crossed the lean features. 'Maybe. I haven't decided yet.' He drew her closer, nuzzling his lips to her cheek. 'I want you!'

A need initiated by another woman, she thought.

'It's early yet,' she said lightly. 'And we haven't danced together for at least a week!'

His laugh was low. 'Not vertically, at any rate.'

'You have a one-track mind,' she accused, adopting the same bantering note.

'So you keep telling me. I think we'll call it a night all the same. Here, at any rate.'

Gina was by no means loath to leave the place. She at least had the satisfaction of seeing Samantha look a little put out when they announced their departure, although the other covered it swiftly with a smile, and a hope to see them again before they returned to LA. Adrian was cordial in his farewells, but made no attempt to echo the sentiment, leaving Gina with the feeling that he might harbour some doubts of his own about that missing hour.

The drive back down the coast in the scented night was pleasurable. She was going to miss all this when they went back, Gina acknowledged. It was doubtful if they'd be visiting the island again. She'd be well able to visit it herself in time to come, of course, but she probably wouldn't. There were plenty of other places to go. Places with no memories to plague her.

Elinor greeted the pair of them with unbridled happiness when they showed up there the day after landing back. She'd so missed having her around, she told Gina. The house had felt so empty.

'I think I might look for something a little smaller, and closer to town,' she said when the three of them were ensconced, as usual, on the terrace. 'An apartment, maybe.'

'I've got a better idea,' Ross put in. 'Why don't you move into the apartment, and we'll take over here? You'll have Room Service on tap when you want it. Maid Service too.'

His mother looked far from turned off by the suggestion, though a little tentative when she glanced Gina's way. 'How would you feel about it?'

Perplexed, she could have told her. Why Ross would want a house the size of this one, she couldn't begin to imagine.

'I'd love it,' she said, unable to see any other possible reply in the circumstances.

'That's settled, then,' Ross declared. 'I'll get things started first thing Monday. I guess you'll want a complete make-over before you move in,' he added to Elinor. 'You never did care for the decor.'

'True enough. I'll get my designer to look at it.' She sounded really enthused. 'You'll want to change things here, too, Gina.'

'I like it exactly the way it is,' Gina answered truthfully, still reeling at the swiftness with which the whole matter was being arranged. 'We have very similar tastes. Are you quite sure about it all?' she felt bound to ask. 'I mean, I know the apartment is big, but it doesn't begin to compare with what you have here. What about the pool, for instance? You swim every morning.'

'The Beverly Harlow has two pools. I'll just make sure I get down there before breakfast.' Elinor obviously had no doubts in mind. She got to her feet. 'I'll go and give Maurice a call. He'll be snowed under as usual, but he'll just have to squeeze me in somehow.'

The pause stretched for several seconds after she'd gone. Ross was the first to speak. 'Any objections?'

'Why would I object?' Gina asked shortly. 'I'd just have appreciated some prior warning.'

'The idea only came to me when my mother mentioned moving,' he said. 'I'd rather keep the place in the family. It will get Meryl and Jack off my back too. They've been on at me to move into the property market for years. I'm sure you'll enjoy living up here better than the apartment.'

She was forced to concede that much. Big as it was, the apartment still felt constrictive in comparison. Probably because the balcony was its only private outside space.

'You really believe your mother will be happy there?' she asked.

'If she already had apartment-living in mind, then yes,' he said. 'She'll transform it anyway. Or Maurice will. She'll have meant what she said about this place too. She won't mind if you want to change things.'

Gina kept her tone steady. 'I don't see much point, considering I'll only be here a few months, at the most.'

The pause was lengthy. When he spoke again it was without particular expression. 'Are you still planning on staying with the company after we finish? Taking an active part, I mean.'

'I doubt it,' she admitted. 'I might go back home to England. Either way, you can have the fifty-one per cent.'

If he was gratified by the offer, it wasn't noticeable. 'What would you do back in England?'

She shrugged. 'Anything that took my fancy, I suppose. I might even travel. Apart from Spain and Italy, and here, of course, I haven't been all that far. I always fancied taking the Trans-Siberian across Russia. Then there's the Great Wall of China, the Taj Mahal, the Valley of Kings.'

'Sounds like a full world tour,' Ross commented drily. 'On your own?'

'The best way to do it,' she said. 'Only myself to please. Anyway, it's just a pipedream at present.'

'It won't be after tomorrow. All we have to do is complete the paperwork. If you're serious about selling me the shares, I'll need another six per cent. We can arrange that at the same time. You'll still retain twenty-four per cent, with a right to draw dividends on it twice a year, whatever you decide to do with your life.'

'Fine.' Gina didn't want to think about it. She'd been talking through her hat with all that guff about touring the world on her own. What kind of pleasure would there be in seeing the sights she had mentioned with no one to share the experience?

The housekeeper came out bearing a round of drinks and some light refreshments on a tray. Her attitude was a little more congenial than it had been in the early days, but Gina still found her difficult to get along with.

'What about staff?' she asked when the woman had gone. 'You'll hardly have need of a chauffeur for a start, and Lydia has never been all that enamoured of me.'

Ross lifted his shoulders. 'Michael does other jobs, and Lydia keeps everything running smoothly. Unless you fancy taking it on yourself?'

She cast a glance at him, disconcerted by his somewhat brusque tone. 'I just thought—'

'It's your choice,' he interposed. 'If you want new people in, have them—if you can find any available. Good, trustworthy staff are like gold here. They can pick and choose jobs.'

Implying that they were fortunate to have the pair at all, Gina took it. There was a possibility that they might decide a change was called for themselves, once it was realised what was to happen—maybe even taking the daily cleaning staff with them. If she didn't want to be left without any help at all, she'd perhaps better start putting some effort into cultivating the relationship.

It took that thought to bring home to her just how far she'd come from the person she'd been two months ago. She'd sworn not to become blasé about her new lifestyle, but she was starting to take certain aspects of it for granted. That stopped right here!

Ross extracted his mobile from a pocket, the expression crossing his face when he glanced at the display unreadable. He must have the set on vibration signal only, Gina thought as he put the instrument to his ear. She preferred an audible tone herself.

'Hi,' he said. 'How are you?' He listened for a moment, then added briefly, 'Afraid I'm tied up right now. I'll ring you later.'

If it hadn't been for the familiar greeting, Gina might have taken it that the call was from a business associate. Suspicion reared its head when he slid the phone back into his pocket without comment, though she did her best to smother it.

Elinor returned looking a little uncertain. Maurice, it seemed, would only agree to tackle the apartment if work could begin right away.

'No problem,' Ross assured her. 'We can move up tomorrow, and leave a clear field. Considering we don't have any furnishings to transport, it shouldn't be too difficult a job. Most of our personal stuff will go in the cars.'

'I can send Michael down with the limo,' his mother offered, carried away by enthusiasm again. 'It's good to know the house will be staying in the family! Oliver would like it too.' She caught herself up as if in sudden recollection, her glance shifting to Gina. 'Sorry, darling, I'm running away with it all. If you need more time...?'

Gina shook her head smilingly, determined not to go for Ross in front of his mother. 'The decision's made. Why wait? We can use my old room for the time being.'

'Oh, no, you'll have the master suite, of course! I'll have Lydia make a start right away.'

Grey eyes met green, the latter smouldering. Ross lifted a quizzical eyebrow, whether genuinely unaware of the reason for her anger, or simply playing dumb, Gina wasn't sure. If she was honest about it, being sidelined again was only a contributory factor. She was almost certain that the phone call had been from some woman.

By the time they left the house at five, everything was arranged. The move would be made the next day, after they'd seen the lawyers.

'So, let's have it,' Ross said when they were on the road. 'I can feel the heat here!'

'I don't like being railroaded!' she said tautly. 'First the house, now the move! This might be a temporary affair, but while we *are* married I expect a say in things!'

There was a dangerous slant to his lips. 'I'll make whatever decisions I think fit, whenever I think fit. As you said a while ago, you'll only be around a few more months.'

It was true, of course, but it still hurt. Damn him! she thought fiercely. Damn this whole farce of a marriage!

The silence was heavy. He reached out and switched on the radio. Gina stole a glance at him, taking in the set of his jaw. That he was good and angry there was no doubt. Well, so was she!

About what exactly, though? came the question. The presumption might spark a certain umbrage, but it wasn't worth getting in a rage about. Neither should she be judging him on the evidence of one phone call she couldn't even be sure was from a woman at all.

He went straight in for a shower when they got to the apartment. Gathering the outer clothing he'd discarded, Gina felt the shape of his mobile in a trouser pocket. Unable to resist the urge, she dialled up the last call received.

The name that appeared above the number displayed was only too familiar: Dione. She put the phone back where she'd found it, chest tight. He'd said he would call back later. To make arrangements to meet, she assumed. She should have left well alone. What the heart didn't know it couldn't grieve over.

As it was to be their last night in the hotel, they had dinner in the Barlborough restaurant. Told of their coming departure, the *maître d'* expressed his regrets, along with his hope that they would continue to dine there occasionally. The senior Mrs Harlow would be well taken care of by everyone, he assured them.

'She'll make sure of that for herself,' Ross observed as the man departed. 'She may come across as easy-going, but heaven help anybody who falls down on a job they're paid to do!'

'I still think she may be making a mistake,' Gina said, finding no reason to hold her opinion when it came to someone she thought a lot of. 'It's so different from what she's been used to.'

'She needs a different environment. The house has too many memories just now.' Ross studied her across the lamplit table. 'Maybe for you too.'

She shook her head. 'I didn't have long enough with Grandfather to develop any. I'll always regret that.'

'His fault, not yours. At least he died knowing he'd done his best to put things right.'

'Yes.' Gina took up her glass, wondering whether the action they were taking to get round his edict would have crossed his mind. It was very possible that Ross was right in saying the tumour must have affected his reason.

'You told me you'd once seen a photograph of my mother,' she said. 'Do you know where it might be now?'

Ross shook his head. 'It was several years ago. I was using the computer in the study, and was looking for more paper for the printer. The photograph was in a drawer. It isn't there now,' he added, anticipating the question. 'I've looked for it. My mother doesn't know what happened to it either, I'm afraid. You do look like her though. Even more so these days.'

'Since I was made over to LA standards, you mean?'

He made a small, impatient gesture. 'I didn't mean it like that, but if it's the way you want to see it…'

Gina bit her lip. They'd only just got back on reasonable terms, now here she was throwing a spanner in the works again. All down to that phone call. So far he'd had little opportunity to make the return call, but there was no doubt in her mind that he would be making it.

She made an effort to put the other woman to the back of her mind. There was nothing to be gained from agonising over her.

The move to Buena Vista went smoothly. Apart from personal items, there was little to transport. By late afternoon they were more or less settled into their new home.

The master suite was the last word in luxury. The sitting room adjoining the bedroom opened via French doors onto a balcony overlooking the fantastic view. From up here, the sea looked closer, reminding Gina that she'd only been out that far once in two whole months. It would take years to become as familiar with the city as Ross himself was. Years she just wasn't going to have.

Elinor had basic plans for the apartment already drawn up. The work was due to start the next day, with completion in four days. Ross reckoned there was no reason why the paperwork dealing with the transaction shouldn't be completed by then.

'The Petersons have agreed to stay on, by the way,' he said that night. 'Although Lydia had some reservations. She seems to think you don't like her.'

'I barely know her,' Gina protested. 'She isn't easy to get to know. I had the feeling from the beginning that she thought I'd no right to be here at all.'

'Are you sure you weren't being a little over-sensitive?' he asked.

Eyeing his reflection through the dressing-table mirror as he lay nude on the bed, she was in no mood for argument. 'Probably so,' she said. 'You do realise it's that time of the month?'

'I didn't, but I guess I do now.' He sounded more amused than disappointed. 'I dare say I can cope.'

More than adequately, she found when she joined him in bed. Lovemaking didn't necessarily have to involve penetration, he said when she reminded him again. He took her to the heights with just lips and tongue, inciting her to respond in kind. Held in his arms later, listening to his steady breathing, she knew she was never going to find another man who could fulfil her the way Ross could. It was a bleak thought.

# CHAPTER TEN

THAT first week went by swiftly. There was a board meeting on the Friday, at which Gina was content to sit back and simply imbibe.

'Things seem to be going well between you and Ross,' Warren Boxhall remarked afterwards, having called in to her office before taking his departure.

'Why wouldn't they be?' she returned. 'We're hardly going to be at loggerheads after three weeks.'

'It's been known,' he said. '*My* marriage went down the pan on honeymoon!'

'Which one?' she asked blandly, drawing a laugh.

'The last one. Last time I venture down the marital road,' he added. 'Too costly.'

'Only when it breaks down. You've obviously never met the right person.'

'I have,' he rejoined, with a mock sigh, 'but just too late.'

Gina was unable to contain a laugh of her own. 'If that's supposed to soften me up, you're way off track. I'm happy with things the way they are.'

'You and Ross might be OK, but we're not all in the same bracket,' he said. 'I've three lots of alimony to find!'

'Be thankful you didn't have children with any of them,' she rejoined, refusing to sympathise.

His sigh this time was genuine. 'You're a hard woman, but I don't give up easily. I'll win you round yet!'

Not in a lifetime, she thought, but she didn't bother saying it.

Ross was lunching with Isabel Dantry again. He hadn't

149

suggested she tagged along, and she wasn't going to suggest it. With capital from the shares she'd let Ross have, she was in a position to start making investments on her own account. What she'd said to Ross about not being interested in increasing her fortune had been baloney, but she certainly didn't see much sense in actioning it until she knew where she was eventually going to finish up.

Eager to show her what had been done to the apartment to date, Elinor had suggested she come over for lunch. Gina hardly recognised the place when they viewed it after eating in the restaurant. The Scandinavian furnishings were gone, the neutral walls in the living room painted a deep green, the stripped-pine floor covered in thickly piled, off-white carpeting. Figured gold drapes had replaced the blinds at the windows.

'I wasn't sure about the colour at first, but Maurice says it will show off my art collection to much greater effect,' Elinor said. 'He's going to position them tomorrow. Sorry to leave so many gaps at the house,' she added, 'but they were all presents from Oliver.'

'They're about the only things you *have* taken,' Gina chided. 'Surely some of the furnishings would fit here too?'

'Not according to Maurice. He demands a free hand throughout.'

'We met someone in Barbados who once did some design work for you at the house,' Gina said casually. 'Samantha Barton?'

Elinor's brow wrinkled for a moment, then cleared. 'Oh, yes! About three years ago. I used her just the once when Maurice was out of the country. She made over two of the bedrooms. Good, though not up to Maurice. Was she there on vacation?'

'She's in business there. Doing very well too, it seems.'

'That's nice.'

It was obvious Elinor had no inkling that anything had occurred between the woman and her son, nor any interest in pursuing the subject. Time she forgot about it herself, Gina acknowledged. Samantha wasn't the problem.

It was gone three when the two of them left the hotel. Too late to bother going back to the office, Gina decided. Not that she'd be missed. Her usefulness to the company was nil at present. She sometimes doubted if it would ever be anything but.

She had a swim with Elinor back at the house, then spent an hour or so basking in the late-afternoon sun. Ross still wasn't home when she went up to shower at six.

He arrived some twenty minutes later, coming straight upstairs.

'Traffic was murderous tonight,' he said, peeling off his jacket. 'Two accidents on Hollywood. How about you? Had a good afternoon?'

'Pleasant,' she acknowledged. 'The apartment's looking very different.'

He laughed. 'I imagine it is.'

'I'm surprised,' Gina remarked, 'that *you* don't want the house restyled.'

'What suits one place doesn't suit another. I've no quarrel with the decor here. As I've said before, there's nothing to stop you from altering it if you want to though.'

'As I've said before, I don't. Apart from a few pictures to cover the holes left by your mother's, it's perfect the way it is.'

'As wives go, you have to be one on your own,' Ross observed drily, already on his way to the bathroom.

As wives anywhere went, she was, she thought acidly. She was wearing a semi-sheer black peignoir over the briefest of black underwear, but he didn't appear to have even noticed. More important things on his mind, she took it.

She was fully dressed when he emerged from the bathroom. He took fresh boxer shorts from a drawer, dropping
the towel wrapping his hips to pull them on. Muscle rippled
beneath the tanned skin of his upper arms and shoulders in
tune with his movements. Gina had an urge to go to him,
to slide her arms about his lean waist and press her lips to
the smoothly tapering back. A week ago she might have
given way. Tonight, she let the momentum pass.

Ross slid his trouser zip, and buckled the leather belt,
eyeing her across the width of the room. 'New dress?'

She held back on the sarcasm, settling for a shake of her
head.

'Looks good on you, anyway,' he commented. 'But then,
you look good in anything. That black item you were wearing when I came in almost stopped me in my tracks!'

'It wasn't noticeable,' she said before she could stop herself, and saw his mouth widen.

'I'd been an hour held up on the freeway. One call out-
weighed the other at the time. Maybe you could wear it
again later.'

'I'm not dressing up just to entice you,' she declared
coolly. 'I may not even feel like it later.'

The glint in his eyes became a gleam, not wholly of
amusement. 'I always did like a challenge.'

'That wasn't…' Gina broke off, holding her hands up in
mock surrender. She should know better by now than to
take him on in a battle of wills. He only had to touch her
to melt any resistance, and he knew it.

Unless he was seeing her in the day, he'd had no opportunity since they moved up here to meet with Dione.
They'd been out to dinner one evening, the others they'd
spent here with Elinor, as they were doing tonight. She was
moving into the apartment tomorrow. There would be no

need for Ross to continue acting the dutiful husband. No reason why he shouldn't stay out all night if he wanted to.

That wasn't the only reason she was going to miss her mother-in-law. They'd become close friends. Elinor was bent on involving her in the charity work she took such interest in herself. Gina was already drawn to it. More, she had to admit, than she was drawn to the world of big business: especially taking her limited time here into consideration. She could at least do some good while she *was* here.

She put the proposition over at dinner, drawing a delighted response from Elinor. Ross's reaction was less easy to define. If it was what she wanted, he said. Obviously, as a major shareholder, she'd still be expected to attend board meetings. Gina could see no real reason for that either, as she was hardly going to be making any useful contribution, but it was only once a month.

'If I'm not going to be here, there's little point getting to grips with the job,' she said later when Ross queried the decision.

'Your choice,' he rejoined expressionlessly. 'Before I forget to mention it again, we're at a première next week. Dione Richards' new film. You'll be needing something special. They're big occasions.'

Gina kept a tight rein on herself. 'Don't worry, I won't let you down.'

It wasn't what he'd meant, as she was very well aware. Unlike most men caught in similar traps, he made no attempt to correct the impression, simply shrugged and left it.

There had been a time when the mere idea of attending a film première would have had her over the moon, she thought as he turned away. If it had been any other film, she might still feel the same, but if it had been any other film, they probably wouldn't be going. Ross wasn't into that kind of function on a regular basis, she was pretty certain.

She'd go, of course. She wouldn't give the other woman the satisfaction of a refusal. But it would take every scrap of self-control she could muster to get her through the event.

Elinor gave no outward indication of finding it a wrench to leave the house she'd shared with her husband for so many years, but Gina wasn't wholly deceived.

'I feel as though we've driven her out,' she said to Ross that evening.

'It was her suggestion that she move in the first place,' he returned. 'The rest made obvious sense.'

'It's all so cut and dried to you, isn't it?' she responded after a moment. 'No room for sentiment.'

'No room for over-emotionalism, for certain.' The glance he turned her way held a hint of impatience. 'I think I can claim to know my mother rather better than you do. If she hadn't wanted to go, she wouldn't have gone. It's as simple as that.'

They'd eaten dinner indoors due to an unexpected late-afternoon shower that had soaked the chair cushions before they could be covered, and were now seated in the living room, neither of them watching the television playing with sound muted. Ross had been out most of the day playing golf, arriving home at six looking out of sorts. Lousy game, he'd said shortly when she asked.

Gina had never played golf herself, and considered losing a game a totally inadequate reason for ill-humour. *If* that was the reason. Lugging around a set of clubs was no proof of a game actually played. Although why would an after-noon spent with Dione put him in a bad mood? she asked herself.

'I suppose we should think about having some people to dinner ourselves now we're on our own,' she said, abandoning the previous subject. 'Maybe eight, counting the two of us. Do you reckon Lydia would cope?'

'She's done it before. My mother entertained on a regular basis before Oliver was diagnosed.' Ross sounded far from interested. 'Who did you have in mind?'

'The Thorntons for certain. They've already had us over here. The others, I'm not too sure. Maybe you should choose.'

He shook his head. 'It's your idea, *your* baby. Just don't make it a birthday party. I'm a mite past blowing out candles.'

'I didn't even know you'd a birthday coming up,' she said. 'Which is it?'

'I'll be thirty-five in a couple of weeks.' His smile was faint. 'Getting on a bit, as they say. When's your birthday?'

'October,' she acknowledged. 'Three more months.'

'I can count.' The irony was heavy. 'If you're thinking we'll be divorced by then, you'd better think again. I'm given to understand that the only way we'll get it through that fast is to go to Reno. Even then, it may not be valid outside the country.'

Gina gazed at him in silence, her mind in a spin. 'How long *will* we have to wait, then?' she got out at length.

The grey eyes held steady. 'The year out, at least.'

'A year!'

His regard sharpened into mockery. 'Afraid you'll just have to accept it. It could be worse.'

Not from where she was sitting, she thought dispiritedly. It was bad enough now living with a man whose only feeling for her was physically orientated. How would it be after a whole year? To say nothing of Dione Richards and her like!

'It doesn't mean *I* have to stay that long though,' she said, grasping at any straw she could find. 'Your mother is the only one likely to be upset by the break-up, but she'd have time to come to terms with it if we started having problems, and decided to take some time apart.'

Ross inclined his head, face impassive. 'Maybe. Let's see how it goes, shall we?'

He shifted his gaze to the open terrace doors. 'It stopped raining. How about a moonlit swim?'

The sudden change of subject left her floundering for a moment. 'It's barely an hour since we ate,' she said at length.

'More than long enough. Especially in water as warm as that out there. I've never used it at night before.'

It would be one way of calming down after the shock he'd just given her, Gina acknowledged.

'I'll fetch suits and towels down,' she said.

'We don't need suits, and there are plenty of towels in the locker down there.' He was already on his feet, extending an inviting hand.

The Petersons had all day Saturday off. Gina knew they'd gone to a concert tonight, and wouldn't be back until late. The thought of sliding into the water unhampered by clothing of any kind was too tempting to resist.

The atmosphere was sultry after the rain. Heated by the sun alone this time of year, the water felt like warm silk on the skin. Gina swam a length underwater, coming to rest on the broad steps leading out from the shallow end. Spread far and wide, the city below was a wonderland of sparkling, multicoloured lights.

'It has its own special beauty, doesn't it?' she said as Ross surfaced beside her.

'So do you,' he returned softly.

He put his hands about her hips, drawing her down into

the water again and pinning her against the side to kiss her with fast rising passion. She allowed her legs to float buoyantly upwards, wrapping them about his waist as he drove to the very centre of her being. His lips burned like fire trailing down the taut line of her throat to find the pulse fluttering in the vulnerable hollow.

She climaxed in shuddering ecstasy, the cry torn from her mingling with his deeper, rougher tone. He made no immediate move to withdraw, cupping her buttocks in both hands to hold her in position, the grey eyes almost black as he looked down into hers. He moved her gently against him, smile deepening as he felt the tremors run through her.

'I always did envy the female recovery rate.'

'You're not doing so badly yourself,' she said unsteadily.

'With the right incentive.'

He kissed her again, more gently than before. His skin was slick beneath her fingers, the muscle dormant for the moment. Gina slid her arms tighter about him as he came slowly back to full, pulsing life.

Later, lying in bed, she went back over the whole evening, trying to work out what she was going to do. The man who'd made love to her in the pool down there had been somehow different—almost tender at times. Maybe there was a chance of deepening the passion he had for her into something worthwhile after all. Maybe...

Her thoughts broke off as Ross turned over in his sleep, his hand seeking her breast. The name he murmured was indistinct, but it certainly wasn't hers.

She chose Versace for the première. Pale gold in colour, it was designed in Roman style, the silver bands wrapping her midriff emphasising both the firm thrust of her breasts and the taut slenderness of her waist. Her hair caught up in a cascade of curls, her make-up flawless, she knew she'd never looked better.

Ross approved the effect wholeheartedly. 'Oliver would have been proud of you,' he said. He took a blue velvet box from his bedside drawer. 'This seems to have been a lucky choice.'

The box contained a necklet of beaten silver, along with matching drop earrings.

'Sheer luck, or a word in your ear from a certain person?' Gina asked as he fastened the necklet for her.

He laughed. 'I might have had a little help.'

'It's perfect anyway.' She turned to slide her arms about his neck and kiss him, eyes emerald-bright. 'You're *so* good to me, Ross!'

If he was aware of the irony, he wasn't rising to it. 'We'd better get going,' he said. 'Mustn't mess up your hair.'

The state of her hair was the last thing on Gina's mind right now, but she had to concede he had a point. While not part of the film world itself, they were still camera fodder by reason of both the Harlow name and the story behind their marriage.

Michael drove them down in the limousine Elinor had decided she no longer needed. He would also be waiting to drive them on to the party after the showing, then later home again. Gina would have happily taken a cab for the latter journey, but Ross didn't suggest it this time.

It was brought home to her just how much interest their story still generated when they alighted from the car at the cinema to recognition from the crowds outside the barriers. Gina doubted if she could have made that walk along the red carpet with any degree of aplomb two months ago; even now, she felt the smile plastered to her face must look utterly phoney. At least she didn't have to pause and wave every few paces, as the stars of the silver screen were doing.

The evening-gowned woman presenter drawing aside some of the arrivals to speak on camera homed in on them as they drew level, refusing to acknowledge any lack of enthusiasm.

'And here we have the couple whose romance set the whole city alight just a few weeks ago!' she announced into the microphone. 'And very well you both look on it! That's a lovely dress, Gina!' She didn't wait for any response—had it been forthcoming—turning her attention to Ross. 'Handsome as any other hero here tonight! Did you ever fancy becoming a film star yourself, Ross?'

'Not since I was seven,' he answered easily, drawing a laugh from the crowd. 'Have a nice evening, Sue.'

Gina stole a glance at him as they moved on into the foyer. 'She's right, you know. You'd make a great cowboy! White hat, naturally.'

'They don't make goody-versus-baddy Westerns any more,' he said. 'And that's enough from you, gal!'

She pulled a face at him, sighing resignedly as flash bulbs popped once more. She had to remember that every gesture, every expression was being captured on camera for public display. There was every chance that some journalist with nothing better to write about would use the grimace as a sign that the marriage was already beginning to break down. Not that it might be such a bad thing at that, came the thought. The rift had to start somewhere.

Sam Walker greeted the pair of them with the familiarity of an old friend. Dione hadn't arrived yet, he said, but they were welcome to go straight through and take their seats if they preferred to escape the TV crews all vying for position.

They did so, to find many rows already well occupied.

Ross chose seats on the end of a row about halfway down the auditorium, welcomed by a couple Gina hadn't met before. Ross introduced them as Anna and Carl Sinden, both part of the production team.

Dione arrived trailing a whole retinue, traversing the aisle issuing extravagant greetings right and left. She looked magnificent in the scarlet gown, Gina had to admit. The glance bestowed on her as the woman passed by was cool, the smile reserved for Ross and Ross alone. He showed no visible reaction, but something tautened ominously in the pit of her stomach.

She sat through the two-hour showing with little idea of the storyline. As Meryl Thornton had once said, Dione wasn't the finest screen actress, but she had a presence that commanded attention. The applause when the credits rolled was loud and prolonged.

'Another box-office hit!' Carl proclaimed with satisfaction. 'Mark was good too, of course, but it's still Dione's vehicle. What do you think, Gina?'

So far as Gina was concerned, Mark Lester was way above Dione's class in the acting stakes, but that wasn't the question being asked. 'Oh, definitely,' she said. 'She's really something!'

Ross gave her a sharpened glance, as if he had caught some discordant note in her voice, but made no comment. Watch the innuendo, Gina warned herself.

The celebration was being held at the studio head's home. A grand old relic from the early twenties, what the house lacked in architectural beauty it made up for in character. The staircase rising from the grand central hall was straight from *Gone with the Wind*, the vast living areas furnished in an eclectic mix of old and new that somehow worked.

There was space and to spare inside, even more of it

outside on the spreading patios. Fringed with palm trees, the free-form pool was a real temptation in the sultry heat: a temptation some of the younger element lost little time in giving way to, with scant respect for the garments they were wearing.

'What can't be salvaged can always be replaced,' Ross commented when Gina remarked on the probable ruination of several designer dresses. 'Those kids have never had to work for what they've got.'

The 'kids' he was referring to were in their late teens, early twenties, but maturity was light-years away, Gina had to agree, if their behaviour was taken into account. Not that anyone else seemed to find the scene reprehensible.

There was dancing both indoors and out, with a regular banquet laid out in a side-room for people to help themselves to. Drawn into a small crowd, along with Anna and Carl, Gina did her best to keep up with a conversation centred on the mechanics of film-making.

Ross had gone to replenish their glasses. Twenty minutes ago, according to her watch. He'd probably got waylaid by someone. She clamped down on the thought that jumped into mind. He wouldn't dare. Not here!

Another ten minutes went by before she finally gave way to the urge beginning to consume her. She made some excuse, and left the people she was with to go back into the house, wandering from room to room in search of her missing husband.

There was no sign of him. Nor was Dione in evidence. There was no closing out the suspicion gnawing at her. The smile Dione had given Ross back at the première had been one of complacency, as if in knowledge of her power to stir him. If they were together now...

Throat tight, Gina forced a smile for the benefit of people around her. Short of searching all the bedrooms, she was left with little choice but to wait for Ross to put in an appearance. Sam Walker collared her, introducing her to the people he was with at the moment. Faced with more film talk, she had difficulty keeping her end up.

She jerked involuntarily when Ross slid his hands about her waist from behind.

'I've been looking everywhere for you!' he said, nodding a greeting to the others in the group. 'I left you outside.'

'About forty minutes ago,' she answered with a lightness purely for effect. 'What happened to the drink you were supposed to be fetching me?'

'I kept getting cornered. I put the glasses down somewhere. Anyway, I see you've been taken good care of.'

'You're a lucky man,' observed one of the older men in the group with somewhat heavy gallantry.

'I know.' Ross removed one hand from her waist, but left the other where it was, urging her gently into movement. 'More than I deserve!'

'You can say that again,' Gina murmured under her breath, and received a querying glance.

'What did you say?'

'I was beginning to think you'd gone home,' she improvised. 'You disappeared so completely.'

'Easy enough to do in this mêlée. Have you had enough yet, or do we stay to the bitter end?'

Gina made no immediate answer, her eyes on the woman who had just come through the double doors from the hall. Dione looked like a cat satiated with cream; she could almost hear the purr. There wasn't a hair on the beautiful dark head out of place, but there would have been time to fix it.

'Oh, definitely stay,' she heard herself saying. 'It's such an experience!'

Ross studied her for a moment, then he shrugged. 'No problem.'

It might be for Michael, waiting with the car, it occurred to her, but she couldn't face being alone with Ross in the back of it right now for fear she'd start throwing accusations in his face. The evidence was purely circumstantial, of course, just as it had been with Samantha, but she was as certain as she could be that he'd been with Dione.

Bored half out of her mind by the endless film talk, she stuck it out till the general exodus got under way around one. Hollywood parties didn't tend to run too far into the small hours: studio days started early. Ross had made no further suggestion to leave, though she'd sensed a growing irritation.

Michael was asleep in the driving seat when they finally got out to the car. Conscience-stricken, Gina was moved to apologise for keeping him waiting so long.

'It isn't at all necessary, ma'am,' he said, looking uncomfortable.

'You embarrassed the man,' Ross said shortly in the car.

'Isn't it the done thing to say sorry to a servant?' she asked, equally shortly.

There was cynicism in his glance. 'He's well paid for what he does. He won't have been sitting there all the time. All the drivers will have been fed and watered round the back.'

'I wasn't to know that,' she defended. 'It just seemed so cavalier.'

'Maybe you should have considered that earlier.' There was a pause, a change of tone. 'Why the sudden yen to stay on anyway? You weren't enjoying it.'

'Into mind-reading now, are you?'

'I can read body language. You've been on edge all

night.' He paused again, eyes on her face. 'Want to try again?'

'Not particularly.' She leaned her head back against the rest, closing her eyes. 'Wake me when we arrive.'

Ross said something short and sharp beneath his breath. He wasn't touching her in any way, but she could feel the anger radiating from him. He could simmer all he liked, she told herself hardily. He could also forget about any lovemaking where she was concerned. And this time she really did mean it!

He was silent for the rest of the journey. Gina thrust open the door and slid from her seat the moment the car came to a stop, heading indoors and straight upstairs without a backward glance. She was tense as a coiled wire when she got to the suite, but single-minded in intent.

She'd expected Ross to follow her, but he didn't. She was in bed when he finally came up more than half an hour later. Wide awake, she lay motionless as he undressed. He used the bathroom, emerging again to come across and slide between the sheets. She could feel his body heat, catch the emotive male scent of his skin.

The silence stretching between them was almost tangible. Gina found herself holding her breath, waiting for something—anything—to happen.

'Go to sleep,' he said brusquely. 'I'm not in the mood either.'

It should have been a relief, but it wasn't. Despite everything, she still wanted him, she acknowledged achingly.

# CHAPTER ELEVEN

THE dinner party proved a successful event. Lydia excelled herself in the catering department, producing four courses *par excellence*, as one guest was moved to remark.

'If you and your husband ever feel like a change, just let me know!' she said shamelessly to Lydia when coffee was brought out to where they sat on the terrace. 'There's a house in the grounds goes with the job.'

'We've always been very comfortable here,' the house-keeper returned. 'But I'll bear it in mind.'

If the latter remark was for her benefit, it made little impact, Gina could have told her. She'd done her level best to get on friendly terms with the woman, but there was still a barrier there.

The men were holding a group discussion on their own. The topic appeared to be golf. Gina wondered how they'd react if she told them to get their asses over here and join the rest of the party.

'You don't golf yourself?' Anna Sinden asked, watching her watching them.

'Never even tried,' Gina acknowledged. 'I realise that makes me something of an oddity here.'

Anna laughed. 'If you are, I am too. Carl plays whenever he possibly can. A good thing we share work, or I wouldn't see much of him. I hadn't realised Ross was an enthusiast too,' she added. 'They must play different courses.'

Or even different games, Gina thought.

'I've given Peter an ultimatum,' declared the woman

who had offered Lydia a job. 'Either I get a bigger share of his time, or I find myself a lover.'

'Has it worked?' asked Meryl.

'Well, we're off on a lengthy cruise the end of the month. The new Queen M. You and Ross should join us, Gina. There were a couple more staterooms still available when we booked last week.'

Peter Rossiter was head of a countrywide store chain, providing June with a multimillion-dollar lifestyle she took entirely for granted. Gina found her likeable enough, but couldn't visualise spending any real length of time in her company. Not that it was likely.

'Nice thought, but I'm planning on taking a trip back to England at the end of the month,' she parried. 'It seems ages since I was there.'

'On your own?' Meryl asked.

The trip had been merely an excuse, though she could hardly admit it in June's hearing. 'I'd think so,' she said. 'Ross has far too much on. Anyone want more coffee?'

Thunder was rolling in the distance when the party broke up around midnight, with occasional electrical flashes lighting up the southern horizon.

'Looks like San Diego's getting it tonight,' Ross observed as the last car pulled away. 'Hopefully, it will keep on moving south.'

He turned back to the house, glancing her way as she fell into step. 'It seemed to go well enough.'

'I think so, yes.'

Gina could think of nothing to add. The past two days had been fraught. For her, at any rate. Ross had made no approach since the other night, but otherwise appeared untouched by the conflict. She'd gathered the impression that any move to restore marital intimacy would have to come from her.

There was a good possibility that she had jumped to the wrong conclusion, she'd been forced to admit. Apart from the phone call Dione had made, she had no concrete evidence that they were in contact at all. One thing she did know: things couldn't go on like this.

'Can we put the other night down to PMS?' she asked, trying to inject a little humour.

Ross lifted a quizzical eyebrow. 'I thought that was only supposed to come just before a period?'

'It is, but I don't have any other excuse for acting up the way I did,' she said. 'I don't know what got into me.'

A hint of a smile flickered across his mouth. 'I know what didn't. I felt decidedly unlover-like that night. Do I take it we're back on good terms again?'

'If you want to be,' she said.

'I think that goes without saying.'

He slid an arm across her shoulders, turning her towards him, face lit by the security light on the wall behind him. Gina met his lips in some relief, resolved to keep her possessiveness in check from now on. They were both free agents. If she wanted to be with him at all, she had to accept it.

Meryl rang after breakfast to say thanks for a great evening.

'Thought I'd catch you before you left,' she said. 'Assuming you're downtown today?'

'Actually, I've backed out.' Gina kept her tone neutral. 'I know the company history from the bottom up, but it doesn't make me of all that much use when it comes to the running of. I've joined Elinor on her charity committee.'

'You know your own mind.' Meryl hesitated. 'About this trip back to England... There's nothing wrong, is there? With you and Ross, I mean. I know the marriage was more or less forced on you both, but you seemed to be making a real go of it.'

Now was the time to admit that the trip had never been a serious proposition, Gina acknowledged, but it was going to sound so anti-June.

'It seems such a long time since I saw my parents,' she said, thinking that was true enough at least.

'Well, don't stay away too long, will you?'

Was there a warning in that last? Gina wondered, replacing the receiver. Did Meryl know something she wasn't prepared to say up front?

She cut the speculation right there before it could expand into something she'd vowed to leave well alone.

Ross had gone back upstairs to get his briefcase. 'What's on your agenda today?' he asked when he came down again.

'Nothing,' she said. 'I might laze around.'

'Why not?' There was no censure in his voice, but no particular interest either, his mind obviously on other matters. 'We've a reservation at Spago's tonight. Seven-thirty. I'll give you a call if I'm going to be late, and you can meet me down there.'

Gina steered clear of the question of what might hold him up, concentrating instead on the fact that he'd made the reservation before they'd made up their differences last night. A small comfort, but a comfort nevertheless.

His parting kiss left her yearning. Not just for more of the same; she'd have been happy to settle for his company alone.

Left to her own devices, she took a book down to the pool deck, discarding it after reading a few paragraphs. Shaded by the wide spread of the umbrella, with a light breeze playing over her body, she had to acknowledge that most people would give a great deal to be doing what she was doing right now. She would be able to do very much whatever she wanted to do for the rest of her life once this was all over. There were other men in the world. Somewhere out there she would find one to take Ross's place, however long she had to wait.

She must have dozed off, waking with a start when someone said her name. Roxanne regarded her with open contempt.

'Enjoying the life you stole from me?'

'Hardly stole from you,' Gina rejoined, gathering her resources. 'You lost it.' She sat up, regarding her sister-in-law with unthrilled eyes. 'Are you alone?'

'If you mean, did I bring the man I was shacked up with, the answer is no,' she said. 'I ditched him a week ago. Where's my mother?'

She obviously didn't know about the switch. It was, thought Gina wryly, going to be another bad shock for her.

'You'll find her down at the Beverly Harlow,' she said. 'We swapped homes.'

'You did *what*?' Roxanne looked stunned.

'Your mother's idea—well, Ross's to start with, but she was all for it.'

'This place, for an *apartment*!'

'With appropriate financial adjustment, of course.' In actual fact, Gina had no idea what adjustment, if any, had been made, but she wasn't about to let Roxanne know that. 'She's had the whole place revamped of course. You won't recognise it.'

'You scheming...' Roxanne broke off, teeth clenching. 'You think you've got it made, don't you?' she bit out. 'All this, and Ross too! Just don't imagine you've got him hogtied in *every* direction!'

'I don't imagine anything.' Gina was having great difficulty hanging on to her temper. 'I think you'd better leave.'

'Oh, don't worry, I'm going.' The tone was scathing now. 'Ross would do whatever was necessary to secure the damned company, but you're no match for Dione, believe me!'

She didn't wait for any response, turning about to head for the steps leading back to the upper levels. Not that Gina had a response ready anyway.

She got up from the lounger and plunged into the pool, swimming end to end half a dozen times in an effort to blank out her sister-in-law's vitriol. It didn't work, of course. All Roxanne had done was underline what she already knew.

The day wore on. Elinor rang mid-afternoon to say Roxanne had paid her a visit.

'It wasn't exactly a mother-daughter love-in,' she observed ruefully. 'How did I manage to bring two such disparate children into the world? I understand she called on you first. I hope she didn't upset you.'

'Not to any degree.' Gina kept her tone level. 'Did she say where she's living at the moment?'

'She still has her apartment in Glendale. Oliver bought it for her when she left Gary. At least, she's no longer with the man Ross spoke to. I asked her about the money she's supposed to owe. She said it was taken care of.'

By her, or by Ross? Gina wondered. If there had ever been any truth in the story to start with.

'I'm glad she's at least back in touch,' she said. 'You must have worried about her.'

'Something I can't help doing, even when it's unappreciated. I'm just thankful not to have the same concerns over Ross.' Elinor briskened her voice. 'How about lunch after tomorrow's committee meeting?'

'Love to.' Gina could at least say that in all honesty.

'See you down here at half after nine, then.'

There was no call from Ross to say he'd be running extra late. She was out of the shower and ready dressed for the evening when he arrived at six-thirty.

'Why didn't you tell me you were planning to go back to England?' he asked without preamble. 'Why leave me to hear about it from someone else?'

'It was just a spur-of-the-moment idea to stop June from going on about joining them on this cruise they're taking,' Gina protested.

'If that was true, you'd have put Meryl right this morning when she called you.'

Green eyes sparked. 'She had no right to call *you* about it!'

'She's concerned. She thinks things might not be all that good between us.'

'I'm sure you reassured her on that point. Assuming you still don't want anyone else to know what we've got planned.'

'It's no one else's business,' he said brusquely. 'I've no objection to you taking a trip back home, just to you not discussing it with me first. I'll make the arrangements.'

Gina swallowed on the sudden hard lump in her throat. Talk about hoist with one's own petard! 'I might think about it in a week or two,' she said, 'but there's too much coming up right now.'

'Fine. Just let me know when you *are* ready.'

So he could plan his own itinerary, she thought as he turned away to start undressing. With her out of the way for a while, he'd be left with a clear field. He might even bring Dione back here.

He'd booked Spago Beverly Hills, not the Sunset Boulevard arm. Gina hadn't been before. For star-gazing, it was reputably among the best in the city. She spotted at least three familiar faces on the way to their table.

It was only after they were seated that she saw Dione across the room. Ross had his back to her, but Gina was sure he was aware of her presence. Though she doubted if it had been a deliberate arrangement, the chances of the woman being here had to be pretty high. Her co-star, Mark Lester, was with her.

She shifted her gaze as the other woman looked across, studying the menu handed to her without taking in a word. She was more than half prepared for the arrival of the *maître d'* at Ross's elbow with an invitation for the two of them to join Miss Richards and Mr Lester at their table, feeling her heart miss a beat when he politely declined without so much as a glance in Dione's direction.

Could she possibly be wrong after all? she wondered. Would he really treat a woman he had feelings for in such a cavalier fashion?

Unless she'd done something to displease him. Dining with Mark Lester, for instance—maybe sleeping with him too. Snubbing her in public the way he just had was the biggest insult he could offer a star of her magnitude. It could mean the affair was over.

Even if it did, it made no difference to his feelings for her, Gina warned herself, but her spirits lifted regardless.

'I'll have the salad to start,' she said on an upbeat note. 'Then the *rhindsgulasch mit spatzle*, whatever that is.'

'Austrian beef stew on pasta.' Ross regarded her speculatively. 'You sound very animated!'

'Hunger,' she claimed. 'I only had fruit at lunch.'

'Not dieting, I hope?' he said. 'You don't need to.'

'Not dieting,' she confirmed. 'I just didn't feel like anything more at the time.'

She wasn't lying about the hunger. Still choked up from

Roxanne's visit, she hadn't actually eaten anything at all at lunch. Buoyed up the way she was at present, she felt she could tackle anything put in front of her.

Dione was still at table when they left the restaurant. Gina couldn't resist glancing her way, to be met by a gaze that fairly glittered with malice. Not that she gave a damn. Ross couldn't be making his indifference clearer. That was what mattered. Right now, it was all that mattered.

He took the surprise birthday party she arranged in good part when it came to the crunch. The beautifully restored E-type Jaguar she had had delivered on the morning drew covetous comment from the men.

'You might try having a word with my wife,' one said to her. 'The best she ever came up with was a bucking-bronco ride for the gym. Nearly broke my back first time I tried it out!'

Ross had received the present with a pleasure allied to some other emotion she'd been unable to deduce. He maybe thought it a bit over-the-top, considering their situation, but she refused to regret the gesture.

He waited until the last guest had left before springing the news on her.

'It's lucky I was here for this. I'm off to New York first thing in the morning. Union problems.'

'Do you have to handle it yourself?' she asked with constraint.

'I'll be taking a couple of people with me, but there are times when it's necessary to bring in the big guns before things blow up out of all proportion.'

'How long do you think you'll be gone?'

'As long as it takes to come to some agreement. A couple of days, maybe more.'

I could come with you, it was on the tip of her tongue

to suggest. She beat the impulse down with difficulty. Even if he'd proved amenable, which was doubtful, she had commitments of her own.

'Why don't you spend a couple of nights down at the apartment?' Ross suggested. 'I know Mother would love to have you.'

'I'll be fine here,' she said, determined not to have him think she couldn't manage without him for a few days.

He took an eight o'clock flight, due in at Kennedy at four-thirty New York time. Allowing him a generous couple of hours to get to the hotel, Gina hoped for a call mid-afternoon—if only to say he'd arrived safely.

It hadn't come when Elinor called at six to suggest she came down to dinner rather than spend the evening on her own. She'd be damned if she'd hang around waiting any longer, she thought irately. He could reach her on her mobile if and when he got round to it.

'A man all over!' her mother-in-law observed, on learning of the omission. 'Oliver was just the same. I remember one time he was gone two whole days before he got round to calling. Could never understand what all the fuss was about.'

They were eating out on the apartment balcony, surrounded by aromatic candles to keep any flying stock at bay. Gina sought a change of subject.

'Do you ever have regrets about leaving Buena Vista? You must miss the view from up there at times, if nothing else.'

Elinor smiled. 'The view from here isn't bad either. This place suits me wonderfully. Big enough to entertain in, and easy to maintain. Needless to say, I rarely use the kitchen. In fact, Maurice has persuaded me to have it taken out and the whole area opened up.

'You should use him yourself when you do get round to making some changes,' she added. 'He's the best there is!'

The most expensive, for certain, Gina reflected. She hardly need concern herself with costs, it was true, but it was a difficult habit to break. In any case, there was no point in making changes to a house she wasn't going to be in for all that much longer.

They'd finished the meal and were relaxing over coffee when her mobile finally rang. Ross came through loud and clear.

'I tried the house. Where are you?'

'With your mother,' she said. 'It must be late there.'

'Eleven-forty,' he confirmed. 'I've been tied up since I arrived.'

Gina caught back the first words that rose to her lips. 'So, how's it going?' she substituted.

'None too good so far. It's going to take a lot of talking to find a meeting point. Are you staying down there after all, then?'

'No.' Gina paused, listening. 'What's the noise I can hear in the background? It sounds like someone laughing.'

'It is. The GM's wife came to dinner with us. We're having a nightcap before turning in. I take it you'll be home if I call again in the morning, then?'

'Yes. Just remember the time difference though. I don't fancy being woken at the crack of dawn.'

'I'll make every effort,' he said drily.

He'd rung off before she could say anything else. Not that there was anything else *to* say. Elinor looked at her expectantly as she put the set down again.

'Bad news?'

'They're having difficulties,' Gina told her.

'Problems, problems, always problems!' Elinor sounded sympathetic. 'Like Oliver, he has to be there in the thick of it. You'll have to start putting your foot down. There's absolutely no need for him to handle everything person-ally.'

'I can imagine his reaction if I tried it,' Gina commented, eliciting a chuckle.

'I said start. It took me years to make any real impression.'

Years she wasn't going to have, Gina thought, descending into depression again.

She made the lengthy drive back to the house without incident. The caller display showed just the one call received at eight thirty-five, minus any message. Ross had called her mobile number at eight-forty——eleven-forty, as he'd said, New York time——and he'd been on line less than five minutes. It had taken him more than five hours to find a slot in which to make those calls.

But then, he'd had far more important things to do with his time.

It was the first night she'd spent alone since the wedding. She slept fitfully, waking at seven feeling far from re-freshed. There was a luncheon in aid of the Cystic Fibrosis Association today. She didn't feel like going, but, having taken all this on, she wasn't going to start crying off.

Due to leave the house by ten, at nine forty-five, with no call as yet from Ross, she could no longer hold out. The hotel number was on file. She asked to be put through to Mr Harlow's suite.

There was a lengthy pause before the man came back on line. 'I'm sorry, Mrs Harlow,' he said courteously,' Mr Harlow isn't in the hotel at present. Do you wish to leave a message?'

Gina declined and rang off, angry with herself for having given way in the first place. It was evident that Ross hadn't given *her* a thought since last night.

The luncheon went off smoothly, raising a substantial sum. Gina had left her mobile switched off during the meal. Switching it on again afterwards, she saw there was a message on her answer phone. Ross sounded remote:

'I tried to reach you at home earlier, but you'd already left. I'll try to speak to you later.'

'Something wrong?' Elinor asked, seeing her expression.

Gina donned a smile. 'Nothing at all. How about doing Rodeo while we're in the area?'

It was gone seven when she finally got home. Michael had fetched the mail in from the box, leaving it stacked on a hall table. Gina went through it swiftly. Most of it was for Ross, but there was one envelope addressed to her for personal attention. Delivered by courier, it appeared.

The single sheet inside proved to be a photostatted copy of a New York newspaper gossip column, with one item marked:

A little bird tells me a certain recently married but still hot-as-they-come hotelier was in town with a starry old flame last night. Can it be that the spark has reignited—or did it never go out?

How long Gina stood there gazing at the cutting, she couldn't have said. It was referring to Ross and Dione, of course. It had to be! The woman she'd heard laughing last night hadn't been the GM's wife at all. Ross had made the call on his mobile, not the hotel landline, as might have been expected. He could have been anywhere.

Whatever his reason for giving Dione the elbow in Spago that night, he'd obviously got over it. Whether she'd discovered he was going to be in New York, and gone there with a view to making up, or had been in the city already, there was no way of knowing. It might even have been arranged, the union meeting a blind. However it had happened, the rift was obviously healed.

With New York over three thousand miles away, she would have known nothing about it if someone hadn't seen fit to send this through. It must have been faxed to a courier office as soon as the paper was published, then brought straight out. The three-hour time difference allowed for it.

The anger sweeping through her allowed no consideration. Enough was enough!

A call to the airport secured her a seat on a flight to La Guardia at nine-fifteen that evening, arriving five-twenty in the morning. She left the house again with just the handbag she'd carried all day, intent on only one thing—confrontation. What happened after that, she neither knew nor cared at present.

Despite the heavy traffic, she was left with almost an hour to wait at the airport until boarding time. She hadn't stopped to change from the lime-green suit she'd attended the luncheon in, standing out by virtue of it amidst the generally more casually clad throng. Catching a glimpse of herself in a mirrored stand, Gina wondered how she could look so outwardly cool and composed when she was such a mess inside.

The flight was long, but uneventful. Cocooned in the reclined first-class seat, she even managed to sleep a little. She spent twenty minutes tidying herself up in the bathroom before they started the descent, shunning all thoughts of retreat. Ross might have no feeling for her other than the physical attraction, but he owed her better than this. If she hadn't agreed to the marriage, he could all too easily have lost the power he set so much store by.

They landed ten minutes early to an overcast day in keeping with her mood. It was still barely six when she emerged into the arrivals hall. A newsstand provided a pre-

vious day's copy of the newspaper named on the fax. There
had been no trickery: the item was there right enough. Not
a column Ross was likely to have perused himself, so he'd
be unprepared.

All to the good, she thought. There was every chance of
finding the two of them together. What she would do if she
did, she had no clear idea as yet.

The hotel reception had several early check-outs already
lined up when she arrived after a cab journey that had
seemed to take for ever. Unwilling to wait, she told a hovering under-manager who she was.

From the expression that swiftly crossed the man's face,
she suspected that if he hadn't actually seen yesterday's
news item, he knew about it. As probably did the whole of
the staff. She kept her head high. Speculation could run riot
for all she cared.

In possession of a keycard to the suite, she ascended to
the tenth floor. She'd altered her watch to New York time
on the plane. It was exactly seven twenty-five when she let
herself into the suite.

The door she took to be to the bedroom stood open, but
there was no sound of movement from within. Little light
either. She went through without hesitation, striding straight
to the window to fling open the heavy drapes.

Jerked awake, Ross rolled over and sat up, shielding his
eyes against the flood of light. Looking at him, Gina felt
the turmoil of the last hours drain suddenly from her as
reason returned. She'd come all this way to face him with
a snippet of gossip that named no names, and may even
have been a plant by her beloved sister-in-law, for all she
knew. Why hadn't she considered that before letting emotion overcome her?

Ross gazed at her blankly for a moment, coming wide

awake as realisation dawned. 'What happened?' he asked urgently.

Throat dry as a bone, she looked for some way out of the situation that didn't involve the truth.

'Nothing happened,' she said. 'I have a couple of days free, so I thought I'd come and join you. Maybe do some shopping.'

'Via the red-eye!'

'It was a spur-of-the-moment decision.' She attempted a laugh. 'Crazy, I know!'

'Crazy isn't the word!' Ross turned his head to look at the bedside clock. 'I ordered a seven o'clock call.'

'Looks like somebody slipped up.' Gina fought to maintain an insouciant note. 'Heads will roll!'

'It's very possible,' he said. 'Who brought you up?'

'No one. I got the key from Reception.'

'Just for the asking?'

'They knew who I was.'

He threw back the sheet and got to his feet, naked as he usually was in bed. 'I need a cold shower. You'd better call Room Service and order breakfast for us both.'

'I already ate on the plane,' she said.

'Then order some for me.'

Gina tried to bring some order to a mind going off at tangents as the door closed behind him. The fact that Dione wasn't with him here in the bed was no actual proof that the item was a plant. On the other hand, he certainly hadn't looked like a man caught out. Thrown off balance for a minute or two, yes.

Shelving the problem for the moment, she went back to the living room, taking off her jacket and slinging it over a chair before picking up the phone to call Room Service. She ordered the full English for Ross, and toast for herself, having lied about eating breakfast on the plane. She could sense the unspoken question from below. Word of her arrival obviously hadn't filtered through to the kitchens yet, though it soon would. Hotel grapevines were second to none, Ross had said once. It seemed a long, long time ago now.

He was wearing suit trousers and a crisp white shirt when he emerged from the bedroom, the pale-grey silk tie slung beneath the collar not yet knotted. Gina had made coffee using the facilities provided. She poured him a cup without bothering to ask, meeting his eyes with a faint shrug, still not certain how to play things.

'You don't need to say it. I shouldn't be here. It was a mad impulse.'

The smile was brief. 'I could think of worse ones. You look remarkably good for someone who travelled all night.'

'An advantage women have in being able to cover the ravages with make-up,' she said. 'Anyway, travelling first class isn't that much of a strain. I ordered full English for you. You can always leave what you don't want.'

'You've changed your tune,' Ross observed ironically. 'Waste not, want not—wasn't that what you told me the night you arrived?'

'You have too good a memory,' she returned. 'Anyway, I was just fighting my corner.'

A knock on the outer door heralded the arrival of Room Service. Gina sat in silence while the trolley was wheeled in and unloaded onto the table in the dining area, meeting the waiter's frankly curious glance with a nod and a smile.

'I suppose he must wonder what I'm doing here,' she murmured after he departed.

'I'm still not all that sure myself,' Ross admitted. 'But as you are, better make the most of it. I'm due at a union meeting at nine, so you'll be doing it on your own. It's likely to be a long process.'

The confirmation that there really was a union problem made an arranged assignation even less likely, she conceded wryly. He mustn't know what had really brought her haring out here. Jealousy was too revealing an emotion.

She took a seat at the table, buttering herself a piece of toast while Ross helped himself to one or two items from the covered hot dishes. He had such wonderful hands, she thought yearningly, watching their movements.

'I don't see any bag,' he remarked, glancing round the room.

'I didn't bring one.' She forced a laugh as his gaze returned to her. 'As I said, a sudden mad impulse! I can buy everything I need.'

Ross shook his head, as if abandoning all attempts at rationalisation. 'Does my mother know about this?'

'No,' she admitted. Neither did the Petersons, she could have added. They would in all probability take it that she'd spent the night at the apartment with her mother-in-law. If she didn't go straight back today, they would need to be given some explanation for her disappearance. After spending most of the day with her, Elinor herself was going to be taken aback, to say the least, by her sudden decision.

'I think you'd better give her a call before she calls out the feds to report a kidnapping,' he said. He studied her, looked on the verge of saying something else, then apparently changed his mind, pushing back his chair to get to his feet. 'We'll talk later.'

'About what?' Gina heard herself ask.

'This whole situation.' He sounded suddenly weary.

He'd left his briefcase on the chair where she'd deposited her handbag on first entering the suite. She watched him as he went to get it, numbly aware that she'd precipitated what could be the beginning of the end. He'd had enough, that

was obvious. So had she, if it came to that. The sooner they
parted, the sooner she got her life together again.

Her handbag toppled off the chair as he took up the
briefcase, falling upside down and spilling its contents on
the carpet. Ross went down on a knee to gather them up.
Fatalistically, Gina saw him straighten the crumpled fax
page she had shoved in the bag last night; saw him come
to an abrupt halt as the marked item caught his eye. She
steeled herself to face him as he straightened.

'Where did *this* come from?' he demanded.

'It was sent to the house some time yesterday,' she said
tonelessly. 'I'm not sure by whom.'

'I've a very good idea,' he said, 'but that can wait. You
took it as proof that I'd arranged to meet Dione here?'

Gina made a resigned gesture. 'Yes.'

'How long have you suspected I was still seeing her?'

She looked at him uncertainly, struck by something in
both tone and expression that didn't jell with what she was
expecting. 'I suppose, all the time.'

'It didn't occur to you to ask me outright?'

'We were each to live our own lives,' she reminded him.
'You'd have told me it was none of my business.'

'Maybe in the beginning. I thought we were past that
stage.'

'Are you saying you haven't been seeing her?' she asked
after a lengthy moment.

'Yes. Not since the wedding, at any rate.'

Gina felt a cautious unfurling begin deep inside. 'Why?'
she whispered.

His lips slanted. 'I'd have thought the answer to that
obvious. I lost interest in her when I fell in love with my
wife.' He shook his head as she made to speak. 'It's all
right. I know you don't feel the same way.'

Gina hardly knew whether to laugh or cry. 'I fell in love

with you long before that,' she said. 'I've been eaten up with jealousy over Dione.' Her voice was husky. 'It's no confidence booster competing with a woman voted the most beautiful in the world.'

'Dione's the product of an industry,' Ross said softly. 'When it comes to natural beauty, there's no comparison.'

Gina went into the arms held out to her, meeting his lips with relief singing through her veins. No more heartache, no more dreading the day they eventually parted. The marriage was real at last.

'You're going to be dreadfully late for your meeting,' she murmured a long time later.

Ross put his lips to her temple where the hair clung damply. 'It can wait. They can all wait! I've far more important matters to attend to right now.'

He looked down at her as she lay beneath him, searching her face feature by feature as though to commit it to memory. 'It never occurred to me that someone with your looks could feel threatened by other women.'

'So little you men know,' she said.

'So it appears.' He was silent a moment just watching her, the look in his eyes a joy to see. 'Whoever sent that fax did us both a favour unbeknowingly. It smacks of Dione's touch, though I wouldn't be surprised if my sister had a hand in it too. They've a lot in common. The reason they get on together.'

'She certainly hates me,' Gina acknowledged wryly.

'You inherited what she thinks should have been hers. She's borne a grudge against me since the day I told her she was responsible for Gary's death.'

'You wouldn't turn your back on her completely though?'

'I wouldn't see her in trouble, no. But she'll be in it up

to her treacherous little neck if she tries any more tricks. She hasn't, has she?' he added, catching the flicker in her eyes.

Gina shook her head, seeing nothing to be gained from telling him about the afternoon Roxanne had caught her by the pool. 'I can deal with anything now,' she said. 'Anything at all!'

He laughed. 'I know the feeling! There were times these past few weeks when I've despaired of it ever coming to this. Especially when you looked so shattered at the thought of a year before we could think about divorce. It wasn't true, anyway. I've no actual idea how long it has to be. I just wanted the breathing space.'

He put his lips to hers again, the tenderness more telling than any passion. '*We* are going to have a long and happy marriage, Mrs Harlow! No more mistrust. I've never loved a woman before. Not in any real sense. Believe me.'

'I do,' she said huskily. 'I feel the same way about you. Dione shot her bolt, and she lost. So did Roxanne. Can we put it all behind us?'

'We already did,' he said.

# HARLEQUIN®
## *Presents*~

**Seduction and Passion Guaranteed!**

Legally wed, but he's never said...
"I love you."

They're...

*Wedlocked!*

**The series
in which
marriages are
made in haste...
and love
comes later...**

**Look out for more Wedlocked! marriage stories
in Harlequin Presents throughout 2005.**

**Coming in May:**
**THE DISOBEDIENT BRIDE**
by Helen Bianchin
#2463

**Coming in June:**
**THE MORETTI MARRIAGE**
by Catherine Spencer
#2474

**www.eHarlequin.com**                    HPWL3

## HARLEQUIN®
### *Presents*
**Seduction and Passion Guaranteed!**

He's got her firmly in his sights
and she's got only one chance of
survival—surrender to his
blackmail...and him...in his bed!

Bedded by...
## *Blackmail*
Forced to bed...then to wed?

**A new miniseries
from Harlequin Presents...**

**Dare you read it?**

Coming in May:
# THE BLACKMAIL PREGNANCY
by *Melanie Milburne* #2468

If you enjoyed what you just read,
then we've got an offer you can't resist!

# Take 2 bestselling love stories FREE!

# Plus get a FREE surprise gift!

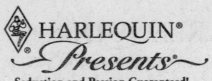

**HARLEQUIN®**
*Presents*

Seduction and Passion Guaranteed!

Introducing a brand-new trilogy by

*Sharon Kendrick*

THE
*ROYAL HOUSE*
OF
*CACCIATORE*

Passion, power & privilege – the dynasty continues
with these handsome princes...

Welcome to Mardivino—a beautiful and wealthy
Mediterranean island principality, with a prestigious
and glamorous royal family. There are three
Cacciatore princes—Nicolo, Guido and
the eldest, the heir, Gianferro.

Next month (May 05), meet Nico in
THE MEDITERRANEAN
PRINCE'S PASSION #2466

Coming in June: Guido's story, in
THE PRINCE'S LOVE-CHILD #2472

Coming soon: Gianferro's story in
THE FUTURE KING'S BRIDE

*Only from Harlequin Presents*

www.eHarlequin.com                    HPRHC

**Seduction and Passion Guaranteed!**

They're the men who have everything—
except brides...

Wealth, power, charm—what else could a
heart-stoppingly handsome tycoon need?
In the GREEK TYCOONS miniseries you have
already been introduced to some gorgeous Greek
multimillionaires who are in need of wives.

**Now it's the turn of favorite Presents
author Lucy Monroe,
with her attention-grabbing romance**

**THE GREEK'S INNOCENT VIRGIN**
Coming in May
#2464

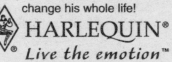